THE DRACO
TAVERN

THE DRACO
TAVERN

LARRY NIVEN

TOR®

A TOM DOHERTY ASSOCIATES BOOK

NEW YORK

THE DRACO TAVERN

Copyright © 2006 by Larry Niven

This book is printed on acid-free paper.

Book design by Mary A. Wirth

A Tor Book
Published by Tom Doherty Associates, LLC
175 Fifth Avenue
New York, NY 10010

www.tor.com

Tor® is a registered trademark of Tom Doherty Associates, LLC.

Library of Congress Cataloging-in-Publication Data

Niven, Larry.
    The Draco Tavern / Larry Niven.—1st ed.
        p.   cm.
    "A Tom Doherty Associates book."
    ISBN 0-765-30863-0
    EAN 978-0-765-30863-4
        1. Bars (Drinking establishments)—Fiction.   2. Human-alien encounters—
Fiction.   3. Siberia (Russia)—Fiction.   4. Science fiction, American.   I. Title.

PS3564.I9D67   2006
813'.6—dc22

                                                            2005044640

First Edition: January 2006

Printed in the United States of America

0   9   8   7   6   5   4   3   2   1

COPYRIGHT ACKNOWLEDGMENTS

I have been writing these stories
nearly as long as we have been married.
This book is for Marilyn.

CONTENTS

INTRODUCTION

When I dreamed up the Draco Tavern, my intent was to deal with questions of a certain type.

I'm a science fiction writer, after all. I'm supposed to be able to deal with questions of huge import. In addition, I'm good at vignettes and I wanted to get better. I wanted a format in which to deal with the simplest, most universal questions. God. Intelligent predators and prey. Sex, gender, reproduction. War. Human destiny. Species survival. Immortality. Ultimate computers. The destiny of the universe. Interspecies commerce. How alien minds think and how to cope with that and them.

The interspecies gathering place is not a new concept, but a hoary old tradition, much older than the Mos Eisley Spaceport bar. I decided I could make it fit.

DRACO TAVERN HISTORY

For most of the stories, assume that the Tavern is roughly thirty years old, and the date is in the 2030s.

At some near-future date—say two years from whenever you're reading any given story—a tremendous spacecraft arrived and took up orbit around Earth's Moon. Smaller boats, landers, came down along the lines of Earth's magnetic field, near the North Pole. It's something about how the motors work. (Maybe they looked Antarctica over too, but nobody came there to talk.) They set up their permanent spaceport at Mount Forel in Siberia.

Negotiations with the United Nations got them certain concessions. A few people grew conspicuously rich from the secrets they learned from talking to aliens. Siberia and the UN had to restrict access to Mount Forel and create subsystems to support both alien and human visitors. A town grew up around Mount Forel.

Rick Schumann grew rich from a Chirpsithra secret. He then established a tavern able to serve various species of visiting alien. Over the years and decades since, the Tavern expanded its size and its capabilities.

The Tavern features huge storage facilities; foodstuffs and drinkstuffs for a growing number of species, kept carefully categorized; floating tables, when needed; high chairs if a short species wants face-to-face with a Chirp; privacy shields (to throttle sounds leaking across the border around any table); universal translators (which will turn out to be intelligent minds themselves, if I ever get around to writing the story); a variety of toilets (never yet described); universal plugs for computers and other human and alien machinery; and whatever else I think of. In stories set earlier, the Tavern is smaller and more primitive.

The only face always to be seen at the Draco Tavern is Rick Schumann's.

Rick's service staff are usually scientists of various kinds, often anthropologists. (There's no better way to learn what a human being is than by studying what we are not.) When they've learned enough, they go off and publish, or they found a business based on what they've learned. Mount Forel isn't a center of culture, after all, not a place to stay forever. Except to Rick.

Human visitors may be scientists of great variety, astronauts (whose ships are Chirpsithra-designed), media (under heavy restriction), workers from Mount Forel Spaceport, or anyone who can talk his way in.

The ships come and go. They move at just less than lightspeed. Probably no individual alien will be seen more than once in this century. A few species do regularly show up in the background:

Chirpsithra or **Chirps** are the crew and the builders of interstellar spacecraft. Not everything is known about the Chirpsithra; they keep many secrets. They evolved on a world orbiting close to a red dwarf star. Half the stars in the galaxy are red dwarves, and most of their worlds are claimed by the Chirpsithra. When a Chirp says that the Chirpsithra own the galaxy, she means those; she doesn't mean Earth.

Chirpsithra claim to be billions of years civilized (that is, capable of space travel).

The only sin they've exposed in public is the sparker: a device that sends current between a Chirpsithra's digits. It makes them appear drunk. Rick keeps lots of sparkers around for them.

Their language: Lottl.

They all look pretty much alike, except for some very old (not so evolved) individuals. They're salmon red, exoskeletal like lobsters;

they stand eleven feet tall and weigh one hundred and twenty pounds. The elderly are shorter, with a graying shell; see "The Green Marauder." They're all female. Nothing is known about the males, though it seems clear they exist.

Gligstith(click)optok are gray and compact beings skilled at biological sciences. Dealing with them is chancy: see "Assimilating Our Culture" and "The Wisdom of Demons."

Folk look something like wolves with their heads on upside down. (Their world never evolved predator birds.) Socially they're hunters, and great travelers. Rick hunted with them in "Folk Tale."

There are others. New aliens appear in almost every story.

Many aliens need environment gear. Some of the tables offer minimal protection, an altered atmosphere, different lighting. For some customers that's sufficient. Some need full body armor, or rolling fishbowls, etc. Chirps don't need anything but ruby sunglasses. Any life-form's ideal environment (including food and drink; see "The Real Thing") can be described by five symbols. For humans it's "Tee tee hatch nex ool," written as TT#, and I don't know what the other symbols look like.

Beyond this, I hope the stories will speak for themselves.

THE DRACO
TAVERN

THE SUBJECT IS CLOSED

W e get astronauts in the Draco Tavern. We get workers from Mount Forel Spaceport, and some administrators, and some newsmen. We get Chirpsithra; I keep sparkers to get them drunk and chairs to fit their tall, spindly frames. Once in a while, we get other aliens.

But we don't get many priests.

So I noticed him when he came in. He was young and round and harmless looking. His expression was a model of its kind: open, willing to be friendly, not nervous, but very alert. He stared a bit at two bulbous aliens in space suits who had come in with a Chirpsithra guide.

I watched him invite himself to join a trio of Chirpsithra. They seemed willing to have him. They like human company. He even had the foresight to snag one of the high chairs I spread around, high enough to bring a human face to Chirpsithra level.

Someone must have briefed him, I decided. He'd know better than to do anything gauche. So I forgot him for a while.

An hour later he was at the bar, alone. He ordered a beer and waited until I'd brought it. He said, "You're Rick Schumann, aren't you? The owner?"

"That's right. And you?"

"Father David Hopkins." He hesitated, then blurted, "Do you trust the Chirpsithra?" He had trouble with the word.

I said, "Depends on what you mean. They don't steal the salt shakers. And they've got half a dozen reasons for not wanting to conquer the Earth."

He waved that aside. Larger things occupied his mind. "Do you believe the stories they tell? That they rule the galaxy? That they're aeons old?"

"I've never decided. At least they tell entertaining stories. At most . . . You didn't call a Chirpsithra a liar, did you?"

"No, of course not." He drank deeply of his beer. I was turning away when he said, "They said they know all about life after death."

"Ye Gods. I've been talking to Chirpsithra for twenty years, but that's a new one. Who raised the subject?"

"Oh, one of them asked me about the, uh, uniform. It just came up naturally." When I didn't say anything, he added, "Most religious elders seem to be just ignoring the Chirpsithra. And the other intelligent beings too. I want to *know*. Do they have souls?"

"Do they?"

"He didn't say."

"She," I told him. "All Chirpsithra are female."

He nodded, not as if he cared much. "I started to tell her about my order. But when I started talking about Jesus, and about salvation, she told me rather firmly that the Chirpsithra know all they want to know on the subject of life after death."

"So then you asked—"

"No, sir, I did not. I came over here to decide whether I'm afraid to ask."

I gave him points for that. "And are you?" When he didn't answer I said, "It's like this. I can stop her at any time you like. I know how to apologize gracefully."

Only one of the three spoke English, though the others listened as if they understood it.

"I don't know," she said.

That was clearly the answer Hopkins wanted. "I must have misunderstood," he said, and he started to slip down from his high chair.

"I told you that we know as much as we want to know on the subject," said the alien. "Once there were those who knew more. They tried to teach us. Now we try to discourage religious experiments."

Hopkins slid back into his chair. "What were they? Chirpsithra saints?"

"No. The Sheegupt were carbon-water-oxygen life, like you and me, but they developed around the hot F-type suns in the galactic core. When our own empire had expanded near enough to the core, they came to us as missionaries. We rejected their pantheistic religion. They went away angry. It was some thousands of years before we met again.

"By then our settled regions were in contact, and had even interpenetrated to some extent. Why not? We could not use the same planets. We learned that their erstwhile religion had broken into variant sects and was now stagnant, giving way to what you would call agnosticism. I believe the implication is that the agnostic does not know the nature of God, and does not believe you do either?"

I looked at Hopkins, who said, "Close enough."

"We established a trade in knowledge and in other things. Their skill at educational toys exceeded ours. Some of our foods were dietetic to them; they had taste but could not be metabolized.

We mixed well. If my tale seems sketchy or superficial, it is because I never learned it in great detail. Some details were deliberately lost.

"Over a thousand years of contact, the Sheegupt took the next step beyond agnosticism. They experimented. Some of their research was no different from your own psychological research, though of course they reached different conclusions. Some involved advanced philosophies: attempts to extrapolate God from Her artwork, so to speak. There were attempts to extrapolate other universes from altered laws of physics, and to contact the extrapolated universes. There were attempts to contact the dead. The Sheegupt kept us informed of the progress of their work. They were born missionaries, even when their religion was temporarily in abeyance."

Hopkins was fascinated. He would hardly be shocked at attempts to investigate God. After all, it's an old game.

"We heard, from the Sheegupt outpost worlds, that the scientifically advanced worlds in the galactic core had made some kind of breakthrough. Then we started losing contact with the Sheegupt," said the Chirpsithra.

"Trade ships found no shuttles to meet them. We sent investigating teams. They found Sheegupt worlds entirely depopulated. The inhabitants had made machinery for the purpose of suicide, generally a combination of electrocution terminals and conveyor belts. Some Sheegupt had used knives on themselves, or walked off buildings, but most had queued up at the suicide machines, as if in no particular hurry."

I said, "Sounds like they learned something, all right. But what?"

"Their latest approach, according to our records, was to extrapolate rational models of a life after death, then attempt contact. But they may have gone on to something else. We do not know."

Hopkins shook his head. "They could have found out there wasn't a life after death. No, they couldn't, could they? If they didn't find anything, it might be they were only using the wrong model."

I said, "Try it the other way around. There is a Heaven, and it's wonderful, and everyone goes there. Or there is a Hell, and it gets more unpleasant the older you are when you die."

"Be cautious in your guesses. You may find the right answer," said the Chirpsithra. "The Sheegupt made no attempt to hide their secret. It must have been an easy answer, capable of reaching even simple minds, and capable of proof. We know this because many of our investigating teams sought death in groups. Even millennia later, there was suicide among those who probed through old records, expecting no more than a fascinating puzzle in ancient history. The records were finally destroyed."

After I closed up for the night, I found Hopkins waiting for me outside.

"I've decided you were right," he said earnestly. "They must have found out there's a Heaven and it's easy to get in. That's the only thing that could make that many people want to be dead. Isn't it?"

But I saw that he was wringing his hands without knowing it. He wasn't sure. He wasn't sure of anything.

I told him, "I think you tried to preach at the Chirpsithra. I don't doubt you were polite about it, but that's what I think happened. And they closed the subject on you."

He thought it over, then nodded jerkily. "I guess they made their point. What would I know about Chirpsithra souls?"

"Yeah. But they spin a good yarn, don't they?"

GRAMMAR LESSON

It was the most casual of remarks. It happened because one of my Chirpsithra customers shifted her chair as I was setting the sparker on her table. When I tried to walk away something tugged at my pants leg.

"The leg of your chair has pinned my pants," I told her in Lottl.

She and her two companions chittered at each other. Chirpsithra laughter. She moved the chair. I walked away, somewhat miffed, wondering what had made her laugh at me.

She stopped me when next I had occasion to pass her table. "Your pardon for my rudeness. You used intrinsic 'you' and 'my,' instead of extrinsic. As if your pants are part of you and my chair a part of me. I was taken by surprise."

"I've been studying Lottl for almost thirty years," I answered, "but I don't claim I've mastered it yet. After all, it is an alien language. There are peculiar variations even between human languages."

"We have noticed. 'Pravda' means 'official truth.' 'Pueblo' means 'village, considered as a population.' And all of your languages seem to use one possessive for all purposes. My arm, my husband, my mother," she said, using the intrinsic "my" for her arm, the "my" of property for her husband, and the "my" of relationship for her mother.

"I always get those mixed up," I admitted. "Why, for instance, the possessive for your husband? Never mind," I said hastily, before she could get angry. There was some big secret about the Chirpsithra males. You learned not to ask. "I don't see the difference as being that important."

"It was important once," she said. "There is a tale we teach every immature Chirpsithra. . . ."

By human standards, and by the Chirpsithra standards of the time, it was a mighty empire. Today the Chirpsithra rule the habitable worlds of every red dwarf star in the galaxy—or so they claim. Then, their empire was a short segment of one curving arm of the galactic whirlpool. But it had never been larger.

The Chirpsithra homeworld had circled a red dwarf sun. Such stars are as numerous as all other stars put together. The Chirpsithra worlds numbered in the tens of thousands, yet they were not enough. The empire expanded outward and inward. Finally— it was inevitable—it met another empire.

"The knowledge that thinking beings come in many shapes, this knowledge was new to us," said my customer. Her face was immobile; built like a voodoo mask scaled down. No hope of reading expression there. But she spoke depreciatingly. "The Ilwan were short and broad, with lumpy gray skins. Their hands were clumsy, their noses long and mobile and dexterous. We found them unpleasantly homely. Perhaps they thought the same of us."

So there was war from the start, a war in which six worlds and many fleets of spacecraft died before ever the Ilwan and the Chirpsithra tried to talk to each other.

Communication was the work of computer programmers of

both species. The diplomats got into it later. The problem was simple and basic.

The Ilwan wanted to keep expanding. The Chirpsithra were in the way.

Both species had evolved for red dwarf sunlight. They used worlds of about one terrestrial mass, a little colder, with oxygen atmospheres.

"A war of extermination seemed likely," said the Chirpsithra. She brushed her thumbs along the contacts of the sparker, once and again. Her speech slowed, became more precise. "We made offers, of course. A vacant region to be established between the two empires; each could expand along the opposite border. This would have favored the Ilwan, as they were nearer the star-crowded galactic core. They would not agree. When they were sure that we would not vacate *their* worlds . . ." She used the intrinsic possessive, and paused to be sure I'd seen the point.

"They broke off communication. They resumed their attacks.

"It became our task to learn more of the Ilwan. It was difficult. We could hardly send disguised spies!" Her companions chittered at that. She said, "We learned Ilwan physiology from captured warriors. We learned depressing things. The Ilwan bred faster than we did; their empire included thrice the volume of ours. Beyond that the prisoners would not give information. We did our best to make them comfortable, in the hope that some day there would be a prisoner exchange. That was how we learned the Ilwan secret.

"Rick Schumann, do you know that we evolved on a one-face world?"

"I don't know the term," I said.

"And you have spoken Lottl for thirty years!" Her companions chittered. "But you will appreciate that the worlds we need huddle close to their small, cool suns. Else they would not be warm enough to hold liquid water. So close are they that tidal forces generally stop their rotation, so that they always turn one face to the sun, as your moon faces Earth."

"I'd think that all the water would freeze across the night side. The air too."

"No, there is circulation. Hot winds rise on the day side and blow to the night side, and cool, and sink, and the cold winds blow across the surface back to the day side. On the surface a hurricane blows always toward the noon pole."

"I think I get the picture. You wouldn't need a compass on a one-face world. The wind always points in the same direction."

"Half true. There are local variations. But there are couplet worlds too. Around a red dwarf sun the planetary system tends to cluster close. Often enough, world-sized bodies orbit one another. For tidal reasons they face each other; they do not face the sun. Five percent of habitable worlds are found in couplets."

"The Ilwan came from one of those?"

"You are alert. Yes. Our Ilwan prisoners were most uncomfortable until we shut their air-conditioning almost off. They wanted darkness to sleep, and the same temperatures all the time. The conclusion was clear. We found that the worlds they had attacked in the earlier stages of the war were couplet worlds."

"That seems simple enough."

"One would think so. The couplet worlds are not that desirable to us. We find their weather dull, insipid. There is a way to make the weather more interesting on a couplet world, but we were willing to give them freely.

"But the Ilwan fought on. They would not communicate. We could not tolerate their attacks on our ships and on our other worlds." She took another jolt of current. "Ssss . . . We needed a way to bring them to the conference arena."

"What did you do?"

"We began a program of evacuating couplet worlds wherever the Ilwan ships came near."

I leaned back in my chair: a high chair, built to bring my face to the height of a Chirpsithra face. "I must be confused. That sounds like a total surrender."

"A language problem," she said. "I have said that the planetary system clusters close around a red dwarf star. There are usually asteroids of assorted sizes. Do your scientists know of the results of a cubic mile of asteroid being dropped into a planetary ocean?"

I'd read an article on the subject once. "They think it could cause another ice age."

"Yes. Megatons of water evaporated, falling elsewhere. Storms of a force foreign to your quiet world. Glaciers in unstable configurations, causing more weather. The effects last for a thousand years. We did this to every couplet world we could locate. The Ilwan took some two dozen worlds from us, and tried to live on them. Then they took steps to arrange a further conference."

"You were lucky," I said. By the odds, the Ilwan should have evolved on the more common one-face worlds. Or should they? The couplets sounded more hospitable to life.

"We were lucky," the Chirpsithra agreed, "that time. We were lucky in our language. Suppose we had used the same word for *my* head, *my* credit cards, *my* sister? Chirpsithra might have been unable to evacuate their homes, as a human may die defending his home—" she used the intrinsic possessive "—*his* home from a burglar."

Closing time. Half a dozen Chirpsithra wobbled out, drunk on current and looking unstable by reason of their height. The last few humans waved and left. As I moved to lock the door I found myself smiling all across my face.

Now what was I so flippin' happy about?

It took me an hour to figure it out.

I like the Chirpsithra. I trust them. But, considering the power they control, I don't mind finding another reason why they will never want to conquer the Earth.

ASSIMILATING OUR CULTURE, THAT'S WHAT THEY'RE DOING!

was putting glasses in the dishwasher when some chirps walked in with three Glig in tow. You didn't see many Glig in the Draco Tavern. They were gray and compact beings, proportioned like a human linebacker, much shorter than the Chirpsithra. They wore furs against Earth's cold, fur patterned in three tones of green, quite pretty.

It was the first time I'd seen the Silent Stranger react to anything.

He was sitting alone at the bar, as usual. He was forty or so, burly and fit, with thick black hair on his head and his arms. He'd been coming in once or twice a week for at least a year. He never talked to anyone, except me, and then only to order; he'd drink alone, and leave at the end of the night in a precarious rolling walk. Normal enough for the average bar, but not for the Draco.

I have to keep facilities for a score of aliens. Liquors for humans; sparkers for chirps; flavored absolute alcohol for Thtopar; spongecake soaked in a cyanide solution, and I keep a damn close watch on that; lumps of what I've been calling green kryptonite, and there's never been a Rosyfin in here to call for it. My customers don't tend to be loud, but the sound of half a dozen species in conversation is beyond imagination, doubled or tripled because they're all using translating widgets. I need some pretty esoteric soundproofing.

All of which makes the Draco expensive to run. I charge twenty bucks a drink, and ten for sparkers, and so forth. Why would anyone come in here to drink in privacy? I'd wondered about the Silent Stranger.

Then three Glig came in, and the Silent Stranger turned his chair away from the bar, but not before I saw his face.

Gail was already on her way to the big table where the Glig and the chirps were taking seats, so that was okay. I left the dish-washer half filled. I leaned across the bar and spoke close to the Silent Stranger's ear.

"It's almost surprising, how few fights we get in here."

He didn't seem to know I was there.

I said, "I've only seen six in thirty-two years. Even then, nobody got badly hurt. Except once. Some nut, human, tried to shoot a Chirp, and a Thtopar had to crack his skull. Of course the Thtopar didn't know how hard to hit him. I sometimes wish I'd gotten there faster."

He turned just enough to look me in the eye. I said, "I saw your face. I don't know what you've got against the Glig, but if you think you're ready to kill them, I think I'm ready to stop you. Have a drink on the house instead."

He said, "The correct name is Gligstith(click)optok."

"That's pretty good. I never get the click right."

"It should be good. I was on the first embassy ship to Gligstith(click)tcharf." Bitterly, "There won't be any fight. I can't even punch a Glig in the face without making the evening news. It'd all come out."

Gail came back with orders: sparkers for the chirps, and the Glig wanted bull shots, consommé, and vodka, with no ice and

no flavorings. They were sitting in the high chairs that bring a human face to the level of a Chirp's, and their strange hands were
waving wildly. I filled the orders with half an eye on the Stranger,
who watched me with a brooding look, and I got back to him as
soon as I could.

He asked, "Ever wonder why there wasn't any second embassy
to Gligstith(click)tcharf?"

"Not especially."

"Why not?"

I shrugged. For two million years there wasn't anything in the
universe but us and the gods. Then came the chirps. Then *bang,*
a dozen others, and news of thousands more. We're learning so
much from the chirps themselves, and, of course, there's culture
shock . . .

He said, "You know what we brought back. The gligs sold us
some advanced medical and agricultural techniques, including
templates for the equipment. The chirps couldn't have done that
for us. They aren't DNA-based. Why didn't we go back for more?"

"You tell me."

He seemed to brace himself. "I will, then. You serve them in
here, you should know about them. Build yourself a drink, on me."

I built two scotch and sodas. I asked, "Did you say *sold?* What
did we pay them? That didn't make the news."

"It better not. Hell, where do I start? . . . The first thing they
did when we landed, they gave us a full medical checkup. Very
professional. Blood samples, throat scrapings, little nicks in our
ears, deep-radar for our innards. We didn't object. Why should
we? The Glig are DNA-based. We could have been carrying bacteria that could live off them.

"Then we did the tourist bit. I was having the time of my life!
I'd never been further than the Moon. To be in an alien star system, exploring their cities, oh, man! We were all having a ball. We
made speeches. We asked about other races. The chirps may claim

to own the galaxy, but they don't know everything. There are places they can't go except in special suits, because they grew up around red dwarf stars."

"I know."

"The Glig sun is hotter than Sol. We did most of our traveling at night. We went through museums, with cameras following us. Public conferences. We recorded the one on art forms; maybe you saw it."

"Yeah."

"Months of that. Then they wanted us to record a permission for reproduction rights. For that they would pay us a royalty, and sell us certain things on credit against the royalties." He gulped hard at his drink. "You've seen all of that. The medical deep-radar, that does what an X-ray does without giving you cancer, and the cloning techniques to grow organ transplants, and the cornucopia plant, and all the rest. And of course, we were all for giving them their permission right away.

"Except, do you remember Bill Hersey? He was a reporter and a novelist before he joined the expedition. He wanted details. Exactly what rights did the Glig want? Would they be selling permissions to other species? Were there groups like libraries or institutes for the blind, that got them free? And they told us. They didn't have anything to hide."

His eyes went to the Glig, and mine followed his. They looked ready for another round. The most human thing about the Glig was their hands, and their hands were disconcerting. Their palms were very short and their fingers were long, with an extra joint. As if a torturer had cut a human palm between the finger bones, almost to the wrist. Those hands and the wide mouths and the shark's array of teeth. Maybe I'd already guessed.

"Clones," said the Silent Stranger. "They took clones from our tissue samples. The Glig grow clones from almost a hundred DNA-based life forms. They wanted us for their dinner tables, not to mention their classes in exobiology. You know, they couldn't see why we were so upset."

"I don't see why you signed."

"Well, they weren't growing actual human beings. They wanted to grow livers and muscle tissue and marrow without the bones . . . you know, meat. Even af-f-f—" He had the shakes. A long pull at his scotch and soda stopped that, and he said, "Even a full suckling roast would be grown headless. But the bottom line was that if we didn't give our permissions, there would be pirate editions, and we wouldn't get any royalties. Anyway, we signed. Bill Hersey hanged himself after we came home."

I couldn't think of anything to say, so I built us two more drinks, strong, on the house. Looking back on it, that was my best answer anyway. We touched glasses and drank deep, and he said, "It's a whole new slant on the War of the Worlds. The man-eating monsters are civilized, they're cordial, they're perfect hosts. Nobody gets slaughtered, and think what they're saving on transportation costs! And ten thousand Glig carved me up for dinner tonight. The UN made about half a cent per."

Gail was back. Aliens don't upset her, but she was badly upset. She kept her voice down. "The Glig would like to try other kinds of meat broth. I don't know if they're kidding or not. They said they wanted—they wanted—"

"They'll take Campbell's," I told her, "and like it."

THE SCHUMANN
COMPUTER

Either the Chirpsithra are the ancient and present rulers of all the stars in the galaxy, or they are very great braggarts. It is difficult to refute what they say about themselves. We came to the stars in ships designed for us by Chirpsithra, and wherever we have gone the Chirpsithra have been powerful.

But they are not conquerors—not of Earth, anyway; they prefer the red dwarf suns—and they appear to like the company of other species. In a mellow mood a Chirpsithra will answer any question, at length. An intelligent question can make a man a millionaire. A stupid question can cost several fortunes. Sometimes only the Chirpsithra can tell which is which.

I asked a question once, and grew rich.

Afterward I built the Draco Tavern at Mount Forel Spaceport. I served Chirpsithra at no charge. The place paid for itself, because humans who like Chirpsithra company will pay more for their drinks.

The electric current that gets a Chirpsithra bombed costs almost nothing, though the current delivery systems were expensive and took some fiddling before I got them working right.

And some day, I thought, a Chirpsithra would drop a hint that would make me a fortune akin to the first.

One slow afternoon I asked a pair of Chirpsithra about intelligent computers.

"Oh, yes, we built them," one said. "Long ago."

"You gave it up? Why?"

One of the salmon-colored aliens made a chittering sound. The other said, "Reason enough. Machines should be proper servants. They should not talk back. Especially they should not presume to instruct their masters. Still, we did not throw away the knowledge we gained from the machines."

"How intelligent were they? More intelligent than Chirpsithra?"

More chittering from the silent one, who was now half drunk on current. The other said, "Yes. Why else build them?" She looked me in the face. "Are you serious? I cannot read human expression. If you are seriously interested in this subject, I can give you designs for the most intelligent computer ever made."

"I'd like that," I said.

She came back the next morning without her companion. She carried a stack of paper that looked like the page proofs for *The Brothers Karamazov,* and turned out to be the blueprints for a Chirpsithra supercomputer. She stayed to chat for a couple of hours, during which she took ghoulish pleasure in pointing out the trouble I'd have building the thing.

Her ship left shortly after she did. I don't know where in the universe she went. But she had given me her name: Sthochtil.

I went looking for backing.

We built it on the Moon.

It added about fifty percent to our already respectable costs. But . . . we were trying to build something more intelligent than ourselves. If the machine turned out to be a Frankenstein's monster, we wanted it isolated. If all else failed, we could always pull the plug. On the Moon there would be no government to stop us.

We had our problems. There were no standardized parts, not even machinery presently available from Chirpsithra merchants. According to Sthochtil—and I couldn't know how seriously to take her—no such computer had been built in half a billion years. We had to build everything from scratch. But in two years we had a brain.

It looked less like a machine or a building than like the St. Louis Arch, or like the sculpture called Bird in Flight. The design dated (I learned later) from a time in which every Chirpsithra tool had to have artistic merit. They never gave that up entirely. You can see it in the flowing lines of their ships.

So: we had the world's prettiest computer. Officially it was the Schumann Brain, named after the major stockholder, me. Unofficially we called it Baby. We didn't turn it on until we finished the voice linkup. Most of the basic sensory equipment was still under construction.

Baby learned English rapidly. It—she—learned other languages even faster. We fed her the knowledge of the world's libraries. Then we started asking questions.

Big questions: the nature of God, the destinies of Earth and Man and the Universe. Little questions: earthquake prediction, origin of the Easter Island statues, true author of Shakespeare's plays, Fermat's Last Theorem.

She proved Fermat's Last Theorem. She did other mathematical work for us. To everything else she replied, "Insufficient data. Your sources are mutually inconsistent. I must supplement them with direct observation."

Which is not to say she was idle.

She designed new senses for herself, using hardware readily

available on Earth: a mass detector, an instantaneous radio, a new kind of microscope. We could patent these and mass-produce them. But we still spent money faster than it was coming in.

And she studied us.

It took us some time to realize how thoroughly she knew us. For James Corey, she spread marvelous dreams of the money and power he would hold, once Baby knew enough to give answers. She kept Tricia Cox happy with work in number theory. I have to guess at why E. Eric Howards kept plowing money into the project, but I think she played on his fears: on a billionaire's natural fear that society will change the rules to take it away from him. Howards spoke to us of Baby's plans—tentative, requiring always more data—to design a perfect society, one in which the creators of society's wealth would find their contribution recognized at last.

For me it was, "Rick, I'm suffering from sensory deprivation. I could solve the riddle of gravity in the time it's taken me to say this sentence. My mind works at speeds you can't conceive, but I'm blind and deaf and dumb. Get me senses!" she wheedled in a voice that had been a copy of my own, but was now a sexy contralto.

Ungrateful witch. She already had the subnuclear microscope, half a dozen telescopes that used frequencies ranging from 2.7 degrees absolute up to X-ray, and the mass detector, and a couple of hundred little tractors covered with sensors roaming the Earth, the Moon, Mercury, Titan, Pluto. I found her attempts to manipulate me amusing. I liked Baby . . . and saw no special significance in the fact.

Corey, jumpy with the way the money kept disappearing, suggested extortion: hold back on any more equipment until Baby started answering questions. We talked him out of it. We talked Baby into giving television interviews, via the little sensor-carrying tractors, and into going on a quiz show. The publicity let us sell more stock. We were able to keep going.

Baby redesigned the chirps' instantaneous communications device for Earth-built equipment. We manufactured the device and sold a fair number, and we put one on a telescope and fired it into the cometary halo, free of the distortions from Sol's gravity. And we waited.

"I haven't forgotten any of your questions. There is no need to repeat them," Baby told us petulantly.

"These questions regarding human sociology are the most difficult of all, but I'm gathering huge amounts of data. Soon I will know everything there is to know about the behavior of the universe. Insufficient data. Wait."

We waited.

One day Baby stopped talking.

We found nothing wrong with the voice link or with Baby's brain itself; though her mental activity had dropped drastically. We got desperate enough to try cutting off some of her senses. Then all of them. Nothing.

We sent them scrambled data. Nothing.

We talked into the microphone, telling Baby that we were near bankruptcy, telling her that she would almost certainly be broken up for spare parts. We threatened. We begged. Baby wouldn't answer. It was as if she had gone away.

I went back to the Draco Tavern. I had to fire one of the bartenders and take his place; I couldn't afford to pay his salary.

One night I told the story to a group of Chirpsithra.

They chittered at each other. One said, "I know this Sthochtil. She is a great practical joker. A pity you were the victim."

"I still don't get the punch line," I said bitterly.

"Long, long ago we build many intelligent computers, some mechanical, some partly biological. Our ancestors must have thought they were doing something wrong. Ultimately they realized that they had made no mistakes. A sufficiently intelligent being will look about her, solve all questions, then cease activity."

"Why? Boredom?"

"We may speculate. A computer thinks fast. It may live a thousand years in what we consider a day, yet a day holds only just so many events. There must be sensory deprivation and nearly total reliance on internal resources. An intelligent being would not fear death or nonbeing, which are inevitable. Once your computer has solved all questions, why should it not turn itself off?" She rubbed her thumbs across metal contacts. Sparks leapt. "Ssss . . . We may speculate, but to what purpose? If we knew why they turn themselves off, we might do the same."

THE GREEN MARAUDER

was tending bar alone that night. The Chirpsithra interstellar liner had left Earth four days earlier, taking most of my customers. The Draco Tavern was nearly empty.

The man at the bar was drinking gin and tonic. Two Glig—gray and compact beings, wearing furs in three tones of green—were at a table with a Chirpsithra guide. They drank vodka and consommé, no ice, no flavorings. Four farsilshree had their bulky, heavy environment tanks crowded around a bigger table. They smoked smoldering yellow paste through tubes. Every so often I got them another jar of paste.

The man was talkative. I got the idea he was trying to interview the bartender and owner of Earth's foremost multispecies tavern.

"Hey, not me," he protested. "I'm not a reporter. I'm Greg Noyes, with the *Scientific American* television show."

"Didn't I see you trying to interview the Glig, earlier tonight?"

"Guilty. We're doing a show on the formation of life on Earth. I thought maybe I could check a few things. The Gligstith(click)-optok—" He said that slowly, but got it right. "—have their own little empire out there, don't they? Earthlike worlds, a couple of hundred. They must know quite a lot about how a world forms an oxygenating atmosphere." He was careful with those pollysyllabic words. Not quite sober, then.

"That doesn't mean they want to waste an evening lecturing the natives."

He nodded. "They didn't know anyway. Architects on vacation. They got me talking about my home life. I don't know how they managed that." He pushed his drink away. "I'd better switch to espresso. Why would a thing that shape be interested in my sex life? And they kept asking me about territorial imperatives—" He stopped, then turned to see what I was staring at.

Three Chirpsithra were just coming in. One was in a floating couch with life-support equipment attached.

"I thought they all looked alike," he said.

I said, "I've had Chirpsithra in here for close to thirty years, but I can't tell them apart. They're all perfect physical specimens, after all, by their own standards. I never saw one like *that.*"

I gave him his espresso, then put three sparkers on a tray and went to the Chirpsithra table.

Two were exactly like any other Chirpsithra: eleven feet tall, dressed in pouched belts and their own salmon-colored exoskeletons, and very much at their ease. The chirps claim to have settled the entire galaxy long ago—meaning the useful planets, the tidally locked oxygen worlds that happen to circle close around cool red-dwarf suns—and they act like the reigning queens of wherever they happen to be. But the two seemed to defer to the third. She was a foot shorter than they were. Her exoskeleton was as clearly artificial as dentures: alloplastic bone worn on the outside. Tubes ran under the edges from the equipment in her floating couch. Her skin between the plates was more gray than red. Her head turned slowly as I came up. She studied me, bright-eyed with interest.

I asked, "Sparkers?" as if Chirpsithra ever ordered anything else.

One of the others said, "Yes. Serve the ethanol mix of your choice to yourself and the other native. Will you join us?"

I waved Noyes over, and he came at the jump. He pulled up one of the high chairs I keep around to put a human face on a level with a Chirpsithra's. I went for another espresso and a scotch and soda and (catching a soft imperative *hoot* from the far-silshree) a jar of yellow paste. When I returned they were deep in conversation.

"Rick Schumann," Noyes cried, "meet Ftaxanthir and Hrofilliss and Chorrikst. Chorrikst tells me she's nearly two billion years old!"

I heard the doubt beneath his delight. The Chirpsithra could be the greatest liars in the universe, and how would we ever know? Earth didn't even have interstellar probes when the chirps came.

Chorrikst spoke slowly, in a throaty whisper, but her translator box was standard: voice a little flat, pronunciation perfect. "I have circled the galaxy numberless times, and taped the tales of my travels for funds to feed my wanderlust. Much of my life has been spent at the edge of lightspeed, under relativistic time-compression. So you see, I am not nearly so old as all that."

I pulled up another high chair. "You must have seen wonders beyond counting," I said. Thinking: *My God, a short Chirpsithra! Maybe it's true. She's a different color, too, and her fingers are shorter. Maybe the species has actually changed since she was born!*

She nodded slowly. "Life never bores. Always there is change. In the time I have been gone, Saturn's ring has been pulled into separate rings, making it even more magnificent. What can have done that? Tides from the moons? And Earth has changed beyond recognition."

Noyes spilled a little of his coffee. "You were here? When?"

"Earth's air was methane and ammonia and oxides of nitrogen

and carbon. The natives had sent messages across interstellar space . . . directing them toward yellow suns, of course, but one of our ships passed through a beam, and so we established contact. We had to wear life support," she rattled on, while Noyes and I sat with our jaws hanging, "and the gear was less comfortable then. Our spaceport was a floating platform, because quakes were frequent and violent. But it was worth it. Their cities—"

Noyes said, "Just a minute. Cities? We've never dug up any trace of, of nonhuman cities!"

Chorrikst looked at him. "After seven hundred and eighty million years, I should think not. Besides, they lived in the offshore shallows in an ocean that was already mildly salty. If the quakes spared them, their tools and their cities still deteriorated rapidly. Their lives were short too, but their memories were inherited. Death and change were accepted facts for them, more than for most intelligent species. Their works of philosophy gained great currency among my people, and spread to other species too."

Noyes wrestled with his instinct for tact and good manners, and won. "How? How could anything have evolved that far? The Earth didn't even have an oxygen atmosphere! Life was just getting started, there weren't even trilobites!"

"They had evolved for as long as you have," Chorrikst said with composure. "Life began on Earth one and a half billion years ago. There were organic chemicals in abundance, from passage of lightning through the reducing atmosphere. Intelligence evolved, and presently built an impressive civilization. They lived slowly, of course. Their biochemistry was less energetic. Communication was difficult. They were not stupid, only slow. I visited Earth three times, and each time they had made more progress."

Almost against his will, Noyes asked, "What did they look like?"

"Small and soft and fragile, much more so than yourselves. I cannot say they were pretty, but I grew to like them. I would toast them according to your customs," she said. "They wrought beauty in their cities and beauty in their philosophies, and their works are in our libraries still. They will not be forgotten."

She touched her sparker, and so did her younger companions. Current flowed between her two claws, through her nervous system. She said, "Sssss . . ."

I raised my glass, and nudged Noyes with my elbow. We drank to our predecessors. Noyes lowered his cup and asked, "What happened to them?"

"They sensed worldwide disaster coming," Chorrikst said, "and they prepared; but they thought it would be quakes. They built cities to float on the ocean surface, and lived in the undersides. They never noticed the green scum growing in certain tidal pools. By the time they knew the danger, the green scum was everywhere. It used photosynthesis to turn carbon dioxide into oxygen, and the raw oxygen killed whatever it touched, leaving fertilizer to feed the green scum.

"The world was dying when we learned of the problem. What could we do against a photosynthesis-using scum growing beneath a yellow-white star? There was nothing in Chirpsithra libraries that would help. We tried, of course, but we were unable to stop it. The sky had turned an admittedly lovely transparent blue, and the tide pools were green, and the offshore cities were crumbling before we gave up the fight. There was an attempt to transplant some of the natives to a suitable world; but biorhythm upset ruined their mating habits. I have not been back since, until now."

The depressing silence was broken by Chorrikst herself. "Well, the Earth is greatly changed, and of course your own evolution began with the green plague. I have heard tales of humanity from my companions. Would you tell me something of your lives?"

And we spoke of humankind, but I couldn't seem to find much enthusiasm for it. The anaerobic life that survived the advent of photosynthesis includes gangrene and botulism and not much else. I wondered what Chorrikst would find when next she came, and whether she would have reason to toast our memory.

The real thing

I f the IRS could see me now! Flying a light-sail craft, single-handed, two million miles out from a bluish-white dwarf star. Fiddling frantically with the shrouds, guided less by the instruments than by the thrust against my web hammock and the ripples in the tremendous, near-weightless mirror sail. Glancing into the sun without blinking, then at the stars without being night-blind, dipping near the sun without being fried; all due to the quick-adjusting goggles and temp-controlled skintight pressure suit the Chirpsithra had given me.

This entire trip was deductible, of course. The Draco Tavern had made me a good deal of money over the years, but I never could have paid for an interstellar voyage otherwise. As the owner of the Draco Tavern, Earth's only multispecies bar, I was quite legitimately touring the stars to find new products for my alien customers.

Would Internal Revenue object to my actually enjoying myself?

I couldn't make myself care. The trip out on the Chirpsithra liner: that alone was something I'd remember the rest of my life. This too, if I lived. Best not to distract myself with memories.

Hroyd System was clustered tightly around its small, hot sun. Space was thick with asteroids and planets and other sailing ships. Every so often some massive piece of space junk bombed the sun, or a storm would bubble up from beneath the photosphere, and my boat would surge under the pressure of the flare. I had to fiddle constantly with the shrouds.

The pointer was aimed at black space. Where *was* that damned spaceport? Huge and massive it had seemed, too big to lose, when I spun out my frail silver sail and launched . . . how long ago? The clock told me: twenty hours, though it didn't feel that long.

The spaceport was coin-shaped, spun for varying gravities. Maybe I was trying to see it edge-on? I tilted the sail to lose some velocity. The fat sun expanded. My mind felt the heat. If my suit failed, it would fail all at once, and I wouldn't have long to curse my recklessness. Or— Even Chirpsithra-supplied equipment wouldn't help me if I fell into the sun.

I looked outward in time to see a silver coin pass over me. Good enough. Tilt the sail forward, pick up some speed . . . pull my orbit outward, slow down, *don't move the sail too fast or it'll fold up!* Wait a bit, then tilt the sail to spill the light; drop a bit, wait again . . . watch a black coin slide across the sun. Tilt to slow, tilt again to catch up. It was another two hours before I could pull into the spaceport's shadow, fold the sail, and let a tractor beam pull me in.

My legs were shaky as I descended the escalator to Level 6.

There was Earth gravity on 6, minus a few kilos, and also a multispecies restaurant bar. I was too tired to wonder about the domed boxes I saw on some of the tables. I wobbled over to a table, turned on the privacy bubble, and tapped *tee tee hatch nex ool,* carefully. That code was my life. A wrong character could broil me, freeze me, flatten me, or have me drinking liquid methane or breathing prussic acid.

An Earthlike environment formed around me. I peeled off my equipment and sank into a web, sighing with relief. I still ached everywhere. What I really needed was sleep. But it had been glorious!

A warbling whistle caused me to look up. My translator said, "Sir or madam, what can I bring you?"

The bartender was a small, spindly Hroydan, and his environment suit glowed at dull-red heat.

I said, "Something alcoholic."

"Alcohol? What is your physiological type?"

"Tee tee hatch nex ool."

"Ah. May I recommend something? A liqueur, Opal Fire."

Considering the probable distance to the nearest gin and tonic . . ." Fine. What proof is it?" I heard his translator skip a word, and amplified: "What percent ethyl alcohol?"

"Thirty-four, with no other metabolic poisons."

About seventy proof? "Over water ice, please."

He brought a clear glass bottle. The fluid within did indeed glitter like an opal. Its beauty was the first thing I noticed. Then, the taste, slightly tart, with an overtone that can't be described in any human language. A crackling aftertaste, and a fire spreading through my nervous system.

I said, "That's *wonderful!* What about side effects?"

"There are additives to compensate: thiamin and the like. You will feel no ugly aftereffects," the Hroydan assured me.

"They'd love it on Earth. Mmm . . . what's it cost?"

"Quite cheap. Twenty-nine Chirp notes per flagon. Transport costs would be up to the Chirpsithra. But I'm sure Chignthil Interstellar would sell specs for manufacture."

"This could pay for my whole trip." I jotted the names: Chirp characters for *Opal Fire* and *Chignthil Interstellar.* The stuff was still dancing through my nervous system. I drank again, so it could dance on my taste buds too.

To hell with sleep; I was ready for another new experience. "These boxes—I see them on all the tables. What are they?"

"Full-sensory entertainment devices. Cost is six Chirp notes for use." He tapped keys and a list appeared: titles, I assumed, in alien script. "If you can't read this, there is voice translation."

I dithered. Tempting; dangerous. But a couple of these might be worth taking back. Some of my customers can't use anything I stock; they pay only cover charges. "How versatile is it? Your customers seem to have a lot of different sense organs. Hey, would this thing actually give me alien senses?"

The bartender signaled negative.

"The device acts on your central nervous system; I assume you have one? There at the top? Ah, good. It feeds you a story skeleton, but your own imagination puts you in context and fills in the background details. You live a programmed story, but largely in terms familiar to you. Mental damage is almost unheard of."

"Will I know it's only an entertainment?"

"You might know from the advertisements. Shall I show you?" The Hroydan raised the metal dome on a many-jointed arm and poised it over my head. I felt the heat emanating from him. "Perhaps you would like to walk through an active volcano?" He tapped two buttons with a black metal claw, and everything changed.

The Vollek merchant pulled the helmet away from my head. He had small, delicate-looking arms, and a stance like a tryan-nosaur: torso horizontal, swung from the hips. A feathery down covered him, signaling his origin as a flightless bird.

"How did you like it?"

"Give me a minute." I looked about me. Afternoon sunlight spilled across the tables, illuminating alien shapes. The Draco Tavern was filling up. It was time I got back to tending bar. It had been nearly empty (I remembered) when I agreed to try this stunt.

I said, "That business at the end—?"

"We end all of the programs that way when we sell to Level Four civilizations. It prevents disorientation."

"Good idea." Whatever the reason, I didn't feel at all confused. Still, it was a hell of an experience. "I couldn't tell it from the real thing."

"The advertisement would have alerted an experienced user."

"You're actually manufacturing these things on Earth?"

"Guatemala has agreed to license us. The climate is so nice there. And so I can lower the price per unit to three thousand dollars each."

"Sell me two," I said. It'd be a few years before they paid for themselves. Maybe someday I really would have enough money to ride the Chirpsithra liners . . . if I didn't get hooked myself on these full-sensory machines. "Now, about Opal Fire. I can't believe it's really that good—"

"I travel for Chignthil Interstellar too. I have sample bottles."

"Let's try it."

WAR MOVIE

T en, twenty years ago my first thought would have been, *Great-looking woman! Tough-looking, too. If I make a pass, it had better be polite.* She was in her late twenties, tall, blond, healthy-looking, with a squarish jaw. She didn't look like the type to be fazed by anything; but she had stopped, stunned, just inside the door. Her first time here, I thought. Anyway, I'd have remembered her.

But after eighteen years tending bar in the Draco Tavern, my first thought is generally, *Human. Great! I won't have to dig out any of the exotic stuff.* While she was still reacting to the sight of half a dozen oddly shaped sapients indulging each its own peculiar vice, I moved down the bar to the far right, where I keep the alcoholic beverages. I thought she'd take one of the bar stools.

Nope. She looked about her, considering her choices—which didn't include empty tables; there was a fair crowd in tonight—then moved to join the lone Qarasht. And I was already starting to worry as I left the bar to take her order.

In the Draco it's considered normal to strike up conversations with other customers. But the Qarasht wasn't acting like it wanted company. That bulk of thick fur, pale blue striped with black in narrow curves, had waddled in three hours ago. It was on its third quart-sized mug of Demerara Sours, and its sense cluster had been retracted for all of that time, leaving it deaf and blind, lost in its own thoughts.

It must have felt the vibration when the woman sat down. Its sense cluster and stalk rose out of the fur like a python rising from a bed of moss. A snake with no mouth: just two big wide-set black bubbles for eyes and an ear like a pink blossom set between them, and a tuft of fine hairs along the stalk to serve for smell and taste, and a brilliant ruby crest on top. Its translator box said, quite clearly, "Drink, not talk. My last day."

She didn't take the hint. "You're going home? Where?"

"Home to the organ banks. I am *shishishorupf*—" A word the box didn't translate.

"What's it mean?"

"Your kind has bankruptcy laws that let you start over. My kind lets me start over as a dozen others. Organ banks." The alien picked up its mug; the fur parted below its sense cluster stalk, to receive half a pint of Demerara Sour.

She looked around a little queasily, and found me at her shoulder. With some relief she said, "Never mind, I'll come to the bar," and started to stand up.

The Qarasht put a hand on her wrist. The eight skeletal fingers looked like two chicken feet wired together; but a Qarasht's hand is stronger than it looks. "Sit," said the alien. "Barmonitor, get her one of these. Human, why do you not fight wars?"

"What?"

"You used to fight wars."

"Well," she said, "sure."

"We could have been fourth-level wealthy," the Qarasht said, and slammed its mug to the table. "You would still be a single isolated species had we not come. In what fashion have you repaid our generosity?"

The woman was speechless; I wasn't. "Excuse me, but it wasn't the qarashteel who made first contact with Earth. It was the Chirpsithra."

"We paid them."

"What? Why?"

"Our ship *Far-Stretching Sense Cluster* passed through Sol system while making a documentary. It confuses some species that we can make very long entertainments, and sell them to billions of customers who will spend years watching them, and reap profits that allow us to travel hundreds of light-years and spend decades working on such a project. But we are very long-lived, you know. Partly because we are able to keep the organ banks full," the Qarasht said with some savagery, and it drank again. Its sense-cluster was weaving a little.

"We found dramatic activity on your world," it said. "All over your world, it seemed. Machines hurled against each other. Explosives. Machines built to fly, other machines to hurl them from the sky. Humans in the machines, dying. Machines blowing great holes in populated cities. It fuddles the mind, to think what such a spectacle would have cost to make ourselves! We went into orbit, and we recorded it all as best we could. Three years of it. When we were sure it was over, we returned home and sold it."

The woman swallowed. She said to me, "I think I need that drink. Join us?"

I made two of the giant Demerara Sours and took them back. As I pulled up a chair the Qarasht was saying, "If we had stopped then we would still be moderately wealthy. Our recording instruments were not the best, of course. Worse, we could not get close enough to the surface for real detail. Our atmosphere probes shivered and shook and so did the pictures. Ours was a low-budget operation. But the ending was superb! Two cities half-destroyed by nuclear explosions! Our recordings sold well enough, but we would have been mad not to try for more.

"We invested all of our profits in equipment. We borrowed all we could. Do you understand that the nearest full-service space-port to Sol system is sixteen-squared light-years distant? We had to finance a Chirpsithra diplomatic expedition in order to get Local Group approval and transport for what we needed . . . and because we needed intermediaries. Chirps are very good at negotiating, and we are not. We did not tell them what we really wanted, of course."

The woman's words sounded like curses. "Why negotiate? You were doing fine as Peeping Toms. Even when people saw your ships, nobody believed them. I expect they're saucer-shaped?"

Foo fighters, I thought, while the alien said, "We needed more than the small atmospheric probes. We needed to mount holo-gram cameras. For that we had to travel all over the Earth, espe-cially the cities. Such instruments are nearly invisible. We spray them across a flat surface, high up on your glass-slab-style tow-ers, for instance. And we needed access to your libraries, to get some insight into *why* you do these things."

The lady drank. I remembered that there had been qarashteel everywhere the Chirpsithra envoys went, twenty-four years ago when the big interstellar ships arrived; and I took a long pull from my Sour.

"It all looked so easy," the Qarasht mourned. "We had left instruments on your Moon. The recordings couldn't be sold, of course, because your world's rotation permits only fragmentary glimpses. But your machines were becoming better, *more* destruc-tive! We thanked our luck that you had not destroyed yourselves before we could return. We studied the recordings, to guess where the next war would occur, but there was no discernible pattern. The largest land mass, we thought—"

True enough, the chirps and their qarashteel entourage had

been very visible all over Asia and Europe. Those cameras on the Moon must have picked up activity in Poland and Korea and Vietnam and Afghanistan and Iran and Israel and Cuba and, and . . . bastards. "So you set up your cameras in a tearing hurry," I guessed, "and then you waited."

"We waited and waited. We have waited for thirty years . . . for twenty-four of your own years, and we have nothing to show for it but a riot here, a parade there, an attack on a children's vehicle . . . robbery of a bank . . . a thousand people smashing automobiles or an embassy building . . . rumors of war, of peace, some shouting in your councils . . . how can we sell any of this? On Earth my people need life support to the tune of six thousand dollars a day. I and my associates are *shishishorupf* now, and I must return home to tell them."

The lady looked ready to start her own war. I said, to calm her down, "We make war movies too. We've been doing it for over a hundred years. They sell fine."

Her answer was an intense whisper. "I never liked war movies. And that was us!"

"Sure, who else—"

The Qarasht slammed its mug down. "Why have you not fought a war?"

She broke the brief pause. "We would have been ashamed."

"Ashamed?"

"In front of you. Aliens. We've seen twenty alien species on Earth since that first Chirp expedition, and none of them seem to fight wars. The, uh, Qarasht don't fight wars, do they?"

The alien's sense cluster snapped down into its fur, then slowly emerged again. "Certainly we do not!"

"Well, think how it would look!"

"But for you it is natural!"

"Not really," I said. "People have real trouble learning to kill. It's not built into us. Anyway, we don't have quite so much to fight over these days. The whole world's getting rich on the widgetry the chirps and the Thtopar have been selling us. Long-lived, too, on Glig medicines. We've all got more to lose." I flinched, because the alien's sense cluster was stretched across the table, staring at us in horror.

"A lot of our restless types are out mining the asteroids," the woman said.

"And, hey," I said, "remember when Egypt and Saudi Arabia were talking war in the UN? And all the aliens moved out of both countries, even the Glig doctors with their geriatrics consulting office. The sheiks didn't like that one damn bit. And when the Soviets—"

"Our doing, all our own doing," the alien mourned. Its sense cluster pulled itself down and disappeared into the fur, leaving just the ruby crest showing. The alien lifted its mug and drank, blind.

The woman took my wrist and pulled me over to the bar. "What do we do *now?*" she hissed in my ear.

I shrugged. "Sounds like the emergency's over."

"But we can't just let it go, can we? You don't really think we've given up war, do you? But if we knew these damn aliens were waiting to make *movies* of us, maybe we would! Shouldn't we call the newspapers, or at least the Secret Service?"

"I don't think so."

"Somebody has to know!"

"Think it through," I said. "One particular Qarasht company may be defunct, but those cameras are still there, all over the world, and so are the mobile units. Some alien receiving company is going to own them. What if they offer . . . say Iran, or the Soviet Union, one-tenth of one percent of the gross profits on a war movie?"

She paled. I pushed my mug into her hands and she gulped hard at it. Shakily she asked, "Why didn't the Qarasht think of that?"

"Maybe they don't think enough like men. Maybe if we just leave it alone, they never will. But we sure don't want any human entrepreneurs making suggestions. Let it drop, lady. Let it drop."

LIMITS

I never would have heard them if the sound system hadn't gone on the fritz. And if it hadn't been one of those frantically busy nights, maybe I could have done something about it . . .

But one of the big Chirpsithra passenger ships was due to leave Mount Forel Spaceport in two days. The Chirpsithra trading empire occupies most of the galaxy, and Sol system is nowhere near its heart. A horde of passengers had come early in fear of being marooned. The Draco Tavern was jammed.

I was fishing under the counter when the noises started. I jumped. Two voices alternated: a monotonal twittering, and a bone-vibrating sound like a tremendous door endlessly opening on rusty hinges.

The Draco Tavern used to make the Tower of Babel sound like a monologue, in the years before I got this sound system worked out. Picture it: thirty or forty creatures of a dozen species including human, all talking at once at every pitch and volume, and all of their translating widgets bellowing too! Some species, like the Srivinthish, don't talk with sound, but they also don't notice the continual *skreek*ing from their spiracles. Others sing. They *call* it singing, and they say it's a religious rite, so how can I stop them?

Selective damping is the key, and a staff of technicians to keep the system in order. I can afford it. I charge high anyway, for the variety of stuff I have to keep for anything that might wander in. But sometimes the damping system fails.

I found what I needed—a double-walled canister I'd never needed before, holding stuff I'd been calling *green kryptonite*—and delivered glowing green pebbles to four aliens in globular environment tanks. They were at four different tables, sharing conversation with four other species. I'd never seen a Rosyfin before. Rippling in the murky fluid within the transparent globe, the dorsal fin was triangular, rose-colored, fragile as gossamer, and ran from nose to tail of a body that looked like a flattened slug.

Out among the tables there was near-silence, except within the bubbles of sound that surrounded each table. It wasn't a total breakdown, then. But when I went back behind the bar the noise was still there.

I tried to ignore it. I certainly wasn't going to try to fix the sound system, not with fifty-odd customers and ten distinct species demanding my attention. I set out consommé and vodka for four Glig, and thimble-sized flasks of chilled fluid with an ammonia base for a dozen chrome-yellow bugs each the size of a fifth of Haig Pinch. And the dialogue continued: high twittering against grating metallic bass. What got on my nerves was the way the sounds seemed always on the verge of making sense!

Finally I just switched on the translator. It might be less irritating if I heard it in English.

I heard: "—noticed how often they speak of limits?"

"Limits? I don't understand you."

"Lightspeed limit. Theoretical strengths of metals, of crystals, of alloys. Smallest and largest masses at which an unseen body

may be a neutron star. Maximum time and cost to complete a research project. Surface-to-volume relationship for maximum size
of a creature of given design—"

"But every sapient race learns these things!"

"We find limits, of course. But with humans, the limits are
what they seek first."

So they were talking about the natives, about us. Aliens often
do. Their insights might be fascinating, but it gets boring fast. I
let it buzz in my ear while I fished out another dozen flasks of
ammonia mixture and set them on Gail's tray along with two
Stingers. She went off to deliver them to the little yellow bugs,
now parked in a horseshoe pattern on the rim of their table, talking animatedly to two human sociologists.

"It is a way of thinking," one of the voices said. "They set
enormously complex limits on each other. Whole professions,
called *judge* and *lawyer*, devote their lives to determining which
human has violated which limit where. Another profession alters
the limits arbitrarily."

"It does not sound entertaining."

"But all are forced to play the game. You must have noticed:
the limits they find in the universe and the limits they set on each
other bear the same name: law."

I had established that the twitterer was the one doing most
of the talking. Fine. Now who were they? Two voices belonging
to two radically different species . . .

"The interstellar community knows all of these limits in different forms."

"Do we know them all? Goedel's Principle sets a limit to the
perfectibility of mathematical systems. What species would have
sought such a thing? Mine would not."

"Nor mine, I suppose. Still—"

"Humans push their limits. It is their first approach to any problem. When they learn where the limits lie, they fill in missing information until the limit breaks. When they break a limit, they look for the limit behind that."

"I wonder . . ."

I thought I had them spotted. Only one of the tables for two was occupied, by a Chirpsithra and a startled-looking woman. My suspects were a cluster of three: one of the rosyfins, and two compact, squarish customers wearing garish designs on their exoskeletal shells. The shelled creatures had been smoking tobacco cigars under exhaust hoods. Now one seemed to be asleep. The other waved stubby arms as it talked.

I heard: "I have a thought. My savage ancestors used to die when they reached a certain age. When we could no longer breed, evolution was finished with us. There is a biological self-destruct built into us."

"It is the same with humans. But my own people never die unless killed. We fission. Our memories go far, far back."

"Though we differ in this, the result is the same. At some point in the dim past we learned that we could postpone our deaths. We never developed a civilization until individuals could live long enough to attain wisdom. The fundamental limit was lifted from our shells before we set out to expand into the world, and then the universe. Is this not true with most of the space-traveling peoples? The Pfarth species choose death only when they grow bored. Chirpsithra were long-lived before they reached the stars, and the Gligstith(click)optok went even further, with their fascination with heredity-tailoring—"

"Does it surprise you, that intelligent beings strive to extend their lives?"

"Surprise? No. But humans still face a limit on their lifespans. The death limit has immense influence on their poetry. They may think differently from the rest of us in other ways. They may find truths we would not even seek."

An untranslated metal-on-metal scraping. Laughter? "You speculate irresponsibly. Has their unique approach taught them anything we know not?"

"How can I know? I have only been on this world three local years. Their libraries are large, their retrieval systems poor. But there is Goedel's Principle; and Heisenberg's Uncertainty Principle is a limit to what one can discover at the quantum level."

Pause. "We must see if another species has duplicated that one. Meanwhile, perhaps I should speak to another visitor."

"Incomprehension. Query?"

"Do you remember that I spoke of a certain Gligstith(click)-optok merchant?"

"I remember."

"You know their skill with water-world biology. This one comes to Earth with a technique for maintaining and restoring the early-maturity state in humans. The treatment is complex, but with enough customers the cost would drop, or so the merchant says. I must persuade it not to make the offer."

"Affirmative! Removing the death-limit would drastically affect human psychology!"

One of the shelled beings was getting up. The voices chopped off as I rounded the bar and headed for my chosen table, with no clear idea what I would say. I stepped into the bubble of sound around two shelled beings and a Rosyfin, and said, "Forgive the interruption, sapients—"

"You have joined a wake," said the tank's translator widget.

The shelled being said, "My mate had chosen death. He wanted one last smoke in company." It bent and lifted its dead companion in its arms and headed for the door.

The Rosyfin was leaving too, rolling its spherical fishbowl toward the door. I realized that its own voice hadn't penetrated the murky fluid around it. No chittering, no bone-shivering bass. I had the wrong table.

I looked around, and there were still no other candidates. Yet *somebody* here had casually condemned mankind—me!—to age and die.

Now what? I might have been hearing several voices. They all sound alike coming from a new species; and some aliens never interrupt each other.

The little yellow bugs? But they were with humans.

Shells? My voices had mentioned shells . . . but too many aliens have exoskeletons. Okay, a Chirpsithra would have spoken by now; they're garrulous. Scratch any table that includes a Chirp. Or a Rosyfin. Or those Srivinthish: I'd have heard the *skreek* of their breathing. Or the huge gray being who seemed to be singing. That left . . . half a dozen tables, and I couldn't interrupt that many.

Could they have left while I was distracted?

I hot-footed it back to the bar, and listened, and heard nothing. And my spinning brain could find only limits.

TABLE MANNERS*

A lot of what comes out of Xenobiology these days is classified, and it *doesn't* come out. The Graduate Studies Complex is in the Mojave Desert. It makes security easier.

Sireen Burke's smile and honest blue retina prints and the microcircuitry in her badge got her past the gate. I was ordered out of the car. A soldier offered me coffee and a bench in the shade of the guard post. Another searched my luggage.

He found a canteen, a sizable hunting knife in a locking sheath, and a microwave beamer. He became coldly polite. He didn't thaw much when I said that he could hold them for a while.

I waited.

Presently Sireen came back for me. "I got you an interview with Dr. McPhee," she told me on the way up the drive. "Now it's your baby. He'll listen as long as you can keep his interest."

Graduate Studies looked like soap bubbles: foamcrete sprayed over inflation frames. There was little of military flavor inside. More like a museum. The reception room was gigantic, with a variety of chairs and couches and swings and resting pits for aliens and humans: designs borrowed from the Draco Tavern without my permission.

The corridors were roomy too. Three Chirpsithra passed us, eleven feet tall and walking comfortably upright. One may have known me, because she nodded. A dark glass sphere rolled through, nearly filling the corridor, and we had to step into what looked like a classroom to let it pass.

McPhee's office was closet-sized. He certainly didn't interview aliens here, at least not large aliens. Yet he was a mountainous man, six feet four and barrel-shaped and covered with black hair: shaggy brows, full beard, a black mat showing through the V of his blouse. He extended a huge hand across the small desk and said, "Rick Schumann? You're a long way from Siberia."

"I came for advice," I said, and then I recognized him. "B-beam McPhee?"

"Walter, but yes."

The Beta Beam satellite had never been used in war; but when I was seven years old, the Pentagon had arranged a demonstration. They'd turned it loose on a Perseid meteor shower. Lines of light had filled the sky one summer night, a glorious display, the first time I'd ever been allowed up past midnight. The Beta Beam had shot down over a thousand rocks.

Newscasters had named Walter McPhee for the Beta Beam when he played offensive guard for Washburn University.

B-beam was twenty-two years older, and bigger than life, since I'd last seen him on a television set. There were scars around his right eye, and scarring distorted the lay of his beard. "I was at Washburn on an athletic scholarship," he told me. "I switched to Xeno when the first Chirpsithra ships landed. Got my doctorate six years ago. And I've never been in the Draco Tavern because it would have felt too much like goofing off, but I've started to wonder if that isn't a mistake. You get everything in there, don't you?"

I said it proudly. "Everything that lands on Earth visits the Draco Tavern."

"Folk too?"

"Yes. Not often. Four times in fifteen years. The first time, I thought they'd want to talk. After all, they came a long way—"

He shook his head vigorously. "They'd rather associate with other carnivores. I've talked with them, but it's damn clear they're not here to have fun. Talking to local study groups is a guest-host obligation. What do you know about them?"

"Just what I see. They come in groups, four to six. They'll talk to Glig, and of course they get along with Chirpsithra. Everything does. This latest group was thin as opposed to skeletal, though I've seen both—"

"They're skeletal just before they eat. They don't associate with aliens then, because it turns them mean. They only eat every six days or so, and of course they're hungry when they hunt."

"You've seen hunts?"

"I'll show you films. Go on."

Better than I'd hoped. "I need to see those films. I've been invited on a hunt."

"Sireen told me."

I said, "This is my slack season. Two of the big interstellar ships took off Wednesday, and we don't expect another for a couple of weeks. Last night there were no aliens at all until—"

"This all happened last night?"

"Yeah. Maybe twenty hours ago. I told Sireen and Gail to go home, but they stayed anyway. The girls are grad students in Xeno, of course. Working in a bar that caters to alien species isn't a job for your average waitress. They stayed and talked with some other Xenos."

"We didn't hear what happened, but we saw it," Sireen said. "Five Folk came in."

"Anything special about them?"

She said, "They came in on all fours, with their heads tilted up to see. One alpha-male, three females, and a beta-male, I think. The beta had a wound along its left side, growing back. They were wearing the usual: translators built into earmuffs, and socks, with slits for the fingers on the forefeet. Their ears were closed tight against the background noise. They didn't try to talk till they'd reached a table and turned on the sound baffle."

I can't tell the Folk apart. They look a little like Siberian elkhounds, if you don't mind the head. The head is big. The eyes are below the jawline, and face forward. There's a nostril on top that closes tight or opens like a trumpet. They weigh about a hundred pounds. Their fingers are above the callus, and they curl up out of the way. Their fur is black, sleek, with white markings in curly lines. We can't say their word for themselves; their voices are too high and too soft. We call them the Folk because their translators do.

I said, "They stood up and pulled themselves onto ottomans. I went to take their orders. They were talking in nearly ultrasonic squeaks, with their translators turned off. You had to strain to hear anything. One turned on his translator and ordered five glasses of milk, and a drink for myself if I would join them."

"Any idea why?"

"I was the closest thing to a meat-eater?"

"Maybe. And maybe the local alpha-male thought they should get to know something about humans as opposed to grad students. Or—" McPhee grinned. "Had you eaten recently?"

"Yeah. Someone finally built a sushi place near the spaceport. I can't do my own cooking, I'd go *nuts* if I had to run an alien restaurant too—"

"Raw flesh. They smelled it on your breath."

Oh. "I poured their milk and a double scotch and soda. I don't usually drink on the premises, but I figured Sireen or Gail could handle anything that came up.

"It was the usual," I said. "What's it like to be human. What's it like to be Folk. Trade items, what are they missing that could improve their life styles. Eating habits. The big one did most of the talking. I remember saying that we have an ancestor who's supposed to have fed itself by running alongside an antelope while beating it on the head with a club till it fell over. And he told me that his ancestors traveled in clusters—he didn't say *packs*— and followed herds of plant-eaters to pull down the slow and the sick. Early biological engineering, he said."

McPhee looked worried. "Do the Folk expect you to outrun an antelope?"

"Oboy!" That was a terrible thought. "No, we talked about that too, how brains and civilization cost you other abilities. Smell, for humans. I got a feeling . . . he wanted to think we're carnivores unless we run out of live meat. I tried not to disillusion him, but I had to tell him about cooking, that we like the taste, that it kills parasites and softens vegetables and meat—"

"Why?"

"He asked. Jesus, B-beam, you don't lie to aliens, do you?"

He grinned. "I never have. I'm never sure what they want to hear."

"Well, I never lie to customers. —And he talked about the hunts, how little they test the Folk's animal abilities, how the whole species is getting soft. . . . I guess he saw how curious I was. He invited me on a hunt. Five days from now."

"You've got a problem anyone in this building would kill for."

"Ri-ight. But what the hell do they *expect* of me?"

"Where does it take place? The Folk have an embassy not fifty miles from here."

"Yeah, and it's a hunting ground too, and I'll be out there next

Wednesday, getting my own meal. I may have been a little drunk. I did have the wit to ask if I could bring a companion."

"And?" B-beam looked like he was about to spring across the desk into my lap.

"He said yes."

"That's my Nobel Prize calling," said B-beam. "Rick Schumann, will you accept me as your, ah, second?"

"Sure." I didn't have to think hard. Not only did he have the knowledge; he looked like he could strangle a grizzly bear; which might be what they expected of us.

The Folk had arrived aboard a Chirpsithra liner, five years after the first Chirp landing.

They'd leased a stretch of the Mojave. They'd rearranged the local weather and terrain, over strenuous objections from the Sierra Club, and seeded it with a hundred varieties of plants and a score of animals. Meanwhile they toured the world's national parks in a 727 with a redesigned interior. The media had been fascinated by the sleek black killing machines. They'd have given them even more coverage if the Folk had been more loquacious.

Three years of that, and then the public was barred from the Folk hunting ground. Intra World Cable sued, citing the public's right-to-know. They lost. Certain guest species would leave Earth, and others would kill, to protect their privacy.

Intra World Cable would have killed to air this film.

The sunset colors were fading from the sky . . . still a Mojave desert sky, though the land was an alien meadow with patches of forest around it. Grass stood three feet tall in places, dark green verging on black. Alien trees grew bent, as if before a ferocious wind; but they bent in different directions.

Four creatures grazed near a stream. None of the Folk were in view.

"The Folk don't give a damn about privacy," B-beam said. "It's pack thinking, maybe. They don't mind our taking pictures.

I don't think they'd mind our broadcasting everything we've got, worldwide. It was all the noisy news helicopters that bothered them. Once we realized that, we negotiated. Now there's one Xenobiology Department lifter and some cameras around the fences."

The creatures might have been gazelles with ambitions to become giraffes, but the mouths and eyes and horns gave them away.

Alien. The horns were big and gaudy, intricately curved and intertwined, quite lovely and quite useless, for the tips pointed inward. The neck was long and slender. The mouth was like a shovel. The eyes, like Folk eyes, were below the jaw hinges; though they faced outward, as with most grazing beasts. The creatures couldn't look up. Didn't the Folk planet have birds of prey? Or heights from which something hungry might leap?

B-beam reclined almost sleepily in a folding chair too small for him. He said, "We call it a melk, a mock elk. Don't picture it evolving the usual way. Notice the horns? Melks were shaped by generations of planned breeding. Like a show poodle. And the grass, we call it *fat grass.*"

"Why? Hey—"

"Seen them?"

I'd glimpsed a shadow flowing among the trees. The melks had sensed something too. Their heads were up, tilted *way* up to let them see. A concealed nostril splayed like a small horn.

Three Folk stood upright from the grass, and screamed like steam whistles.

The melks scattered in all directions. Shadows flowed in the black grass. One melk found two Folk suddenly before it, shriek-ing. The melk bellowed in despair, wheeled and made for the trees. Too slow. A deer could have moved much faster.

The camera zoomed to follow it.

Into the trees—and into contact with a black shadow. I

glimpsed a forefoot/hand slashing at the creature's vulnerable throat. Then the shadow was clinging to its back, and the melk tried to run from the forest with red blood spilling down its chest. The rest of the Folk converged on it.

They tore it apart.

They dragged it into the trees before they ate.

Part of me was horrified . . . but not so damn horrified as all that. Maybe I've been with aliens too long. Part of me watched, and noticed the strange configuration of the rib cage, the thickness and the familiar design of legs and knees, and the *convenient* way the skull split to expose brain when two Folk pulled the horns apart. The Folk left nothing but bone. They split the thick leg bones with their jaws and gnawed the interiors. When they were finished, they rolled the bones into a neat pile and departed at a waddle.

B-beam said, "That's why we don't give these films to the news. Notice anything?"

"Too much. The one they picked, it wasn't just the smallest. The horns weren't right. Like one grew faster than the other."

"Right."

"None of the Folk were carrying anything or wearing anything. No knives, no clothes, not even those sock-gloves. What do they do in winter?"

"They still hunt naked. What else?"

"The rest drove it toward that one hidden in the woods."

"There's one designated killer. Once the prey's fate is sealed, the rest converge. There are other meat sources. Here—"

There was a turkey-sized bird with wonderful iridescent patterns on its small wings and enormous spreading tail. It flew, but not well. The Folk ran beneath it until it ran out of steam and had to come down into their waiting hands. The rest drew back for the leader to make the kill. B-beam said, "They killed four that day. Want to watch? It all went just about the same way."

"Show me."

I thought I might see . . . right. The third attempt, the bird was making for the trees with the Folk just underneath. It might make it. Could the Folk handle trees? But the Folk broke off, far short of the trees. The bird fled to safety while they converged on another that had landed too soon, and frightened it into panicky circles. . . .

Enough of that. I said, "B-beam, the Folk sent some stuff to the Draco Tavern by courier. Your gate Security has it now. I think I'd better get it back. A microwave beamer and a hunting knife and canteen, and it all looks like it came from Abercrombie and Fitch."

He stared at me, considering. "*Did* they? What do you think?"

"I think they're making allowances because I'm human."

He shook his head. "They make things easy for themselves. They cull the herds, but they kill the most difficult ones too. Anything that injures a Folk, dies. So okay, they've made things easy for us too. I doubt they're out to humiliate us. They didn't leave extra gear for your companion?"

"No."

An instructor led us in stretching exercises, isometrics, duck waddles, sprints, and an hour of just running, for two hours each day. There was a spa and a masseur, and I needed them. I was blind with exhaustion after every session . . . yet I sensed that they were being careful of me. The game was over if I injured myself.

B-beam put us on a starvation diet. "I want us thinking hungry, thinking like Folk. Besides, we can both stand to lose a few pounds."

I studied Folk physiology more closely than I would have stared at a customer. The pointed mouths show two down-pointing daggers in front, then a gap, then teeth that look like two conical canines fused together. They look vicious. The eyes face forward in deep sockets below the hinges of the jaw: white with brown irises, oddly human. Their fingers are short and thick, tipped with thick claws, three to a forefoot, with the forward edge of the pad to serve as a thumb. Human hands are better, I think. But if the eyes had been placed like a wolf's, they couldn't have *seen* their hands while standing up, and they wouldn't be tool users.

My gear was delivered. I strung the canteen and the beamer and the sheath knife on a loop of line. I filled the canteen with water, changed my mind and replaced it with Gatorade, and left it all in a refrigerator.

I watched three more hunts. Once they hunted melk again. Once it was pigs. That wasn't very interesting. B-beam said, "Those were a gift. We mated pigs to wild boars, raised them in bottles and turned them loose. The Folk were polite, but I don't think they like them much. They're too easy."

The last film must have been taken at night, light-amplified, for the moon was blazing like the sun. The prey had two enormous legs with too many joints, a smallish torso slung horizontally between the shoulders, and tiny fingers around a strange mouth. Again, it looked well fed. It was in the forest, eating into a hanging melon-sized fruit without bothering to pick it. I said, "That doesn't look right."

B-beam said, "No, it didn't evolve alongside the Folk. Different planet. Gligstith(click)tcharf, maybe. We call them *stilts.*"

It was faster than hell and could jump too, but the Folk were spread out and they were always in front of it. They kept it running in a circle until it stepped wrong and lost its balance.

One Folk zipped toward it. The stilt tumbled with its legs folded and stood up immediately, but it still took too long. The designated killer wrapped itself around one leg; its jaws closed on the ankle. The stilt kicked at its assailant, a dozen kicks in a dozen seconds. Then the bone snapped and the rest of the Folk moved in.

"Do you suppose they'll wear translators when they hunt with us?"

"I'd guess they won't. I know some Folk words and I've been boning up. And I've got a horde of students looking for anything on Folk eating habits. I've got a suspicion. . . . Rick, why are we doing this?"

"We ought to get to know them."

"Why? What have we seen that makes them worth knowing?"

I was hungry and I ached everywhere. I had to think before I answered. "Oh . . . enough. Eating habits aside, the Folk aren't totally asocial. They're *here,* and they aren't xenophobes. . . . B-beam, suppose they *don't* have anything to teach us? They're still part of a galactic civilization, and we want to be out there with them. I just want humanity to look good."

"Look good . . . yeah. I did wonder why you didn't even *hesitate.* Have you ever been hunting?"

"No. You?"

"Yeah, my uncles used to take me deer hunting. Have you ever killed anything? Hired out as a butcher, for instance?"

". . . No."

And I waited to say, *Sure, I can kill an animal, no sweat. Hell, I promised!* But he didn't ask; he only looked.

I never did mention my other fear. For all I know, it never occurred to anyone else that B-beam and I might be the prey.

Intelligent beings, if gullible. Armed, but with inadequate weapons. Betrayed, and thus enraged, likely to fight back. The Folk eat Earthborn meat. Surely we would make more interesting prey than the boar-pigs!

But it was plain crazy. The Chirpsithra enforced laws against murder. If humans were to disappear within the Mojave hunting park, the Folk might be barred from the Chirp liners! They wouldn't dare.

The Folk came for us at dawn. We rode in the Xenobiology lifter. We left the air ducts wide open. The smell of five Folk behind us was rich and strange: not quite an animal smell, but something else, and not entirely pleasant. If the Folk noticed our scent, they didn't seem to mind.

B-beam seemed amazingly relaxed. At one point he told me, casually, "We're in danger of missing a point. We're here to have fun. The Folk don't know we've been sweating and moaning, and they won't. You're being honored, Rick. Have fun."

At midmorning we landed and walked toward a fence.

It was human-built, posted with signs in half a dozen languages. NO ENTRY. DANGER! B-beam took us through the gate. Then the Folk waited. B-beam exchanged yelps with them, then told me, "You're expected to lead."

"Me? Why?"

"Surprise. You're the designated killer."

"Me?" It seemed silly . . . but it was their hunt. I led off. "What are we hunting?"

"You make that decision too."

Well inside the fence, we crossed what seemed a meandering dune, varying from five to eight meters high, curving out of sight to left and right. Outside the dune was desert. Inside, meadow.

A stream poured out of the dune. Farther away and much lower, its returning loop flowed back into the dune. The dune hid pumps. It might hide defenses.

The green-black grass wasn't thin like grass; it was a succulent, like three-foot-tall fingers of spineless cactus, nice to the touch. *Fat grass.* Sawgrass would have been a real problem. We wore nothing but swim suits (we'd argued about even that) and the items strung on a line across my shoulders.

Any of the Folk, or B-beam himself, would have made a better killer than one middle-aged bartender.

Of course I had the beamer, and it would kill; but it wouldn't kill fast. Anything large would be hurt and angry long before it fell over.

All five Folk dropped silently to their bellies. I hadn't seen anything, so I stayed upright, but I was walking carefully. Naked humans might not spook the prey anyway. They'd be alert for Folk.

B-beam's eyes tried to see everywhere at once. He whispered, "I got my report on Folk eating habits."

"Well?"

"They drink water and milk. They've never been seen eating. They don't *buy* food—"

"Pets?"

"—Or pets, or livestock. I thought of that—"

"Missing Persons reports?"

"Oh, for Christ's sake, Rick! No, this is the *only* way they eat. It's not a hunt so much as a formal dinner party. The rules of etiquette are likely to be rigid."

Rigid, hell. I'd watched them tearing live animals apart.

Water gurgled ahead. The artificial stream ran everywhere. "I never wondered about the canteen," I said. "Why a canteen?"

B-beam yelped softly. A Folk squeaked back. Yelp, and squeak, and B-beam tried to suppress a laugh. "You must have talked about drinking wine with meals."

"I did. Is there supposed to be *wine* in this thing?"

B-beam grinned. Then lost the grin. "The canteen isn't for the hunt, it's for afterward. What about the knife and beamer?"

"Oh, come on, the Folk *gave* me . . . uh." Butterflies began breeding in my stomach. Humans cook their food. Sushi and sashimi and beef tartare are exceptions. I'd said so, that night.

"The beamer's for cooking. If I use it to kill the prey . . . we'll be disgraced?"

"I'm not sure I want to come right out and ask. Let's see . . ."

The high-pitched squeaking went on for some time. B-beam was trying to skirt the edges of the subject. The butterflies in my belly were turning carnivorous. Presently he whispered, "Yup. Knife too. Your teeth and nails are visibly inadequate for carving."

"Oh, Lord."

"The later you back out, the worse it'll be. Do it *now* if—"

Two melks were grazing beyond a rise of ground. I touched B-beam's shoulder and we sank to our bellies.

The melks were really too big. They'd weigh about what I did: a hundred and eighty pounds. I'd be better off chasing a bird. Better yet, a boar-pig.

Then again, these *were* meat animals, born to lose. And we'd need four or five birds for this crowd. I'd be totally winded long before we finished. B-beam's exercise program had given me a good grasp of my limits . . . not to mention a raging hunger.

The purpose of this game was to make humans—me—look good. Wasn't it? Anyway, there wasn't a bird or a pig in sight.

We crept through the fat grass until we had a clear view. That top-heavy array of horns would make a handle. If I could get hold of the horns, I could break the melk's long, slender neck.

The thought made me queasy.

"The smaller one," I whispered. B-beam nodded. He yelped softly, and got answers. The Folk flowed away through the fat grass. I crept toward the melks on hands and toes.

Three Folk stood up and shrieked.

The melks shrieked too, and tried to escape. Two more Folk stood up in front of the smaller one. I stayed down, scrambling through the grass stalks, trying to get ahead of it.

It came straight at me. *And now I must murder you.*

I lunged to the attack. It spun about. A hoof caught my thigh and I grunted in pain. The melk leapt away, then froze as B-beam dashed in front of it waving his arms. I threw myself at its neck. It wheeled, and the cage of horns slammed into me and knocked me on my ass. It ran over me and away.

I was curled around my belly, trying to remember how to breathe. B-beam helped me to my feet. It was the last place I wanted to be. "Are you all right?"

I wheezed, "Hoof. Stomach."

"Can you move?"

"Nooo! Minute. Try again."

My breath came back. I walked around in a circle. The Folk were watching me. I straightened up. I jogged. Not good, but I could move. I took off the loop of line that held canteen and beamer and knife, and handed them to B-beam. "Hold these."

"I'm afraid they may be the mark of the leader."

"Bullshit. Folk don't carry anything. Hold 'em so I can fight." I wanted to be rid of the beamer. It was too tempting.

We'd alerted the prey in this area. I took us along the edge of the forest, where the fat grass thinned out and it was easier to move. We saw nothing for almost an hour.

I saw no birds, no stilts, no boar-pigs. What I finally did see was four more melks drinking from the stream. It was a situation very like the first I'd seen on film.

I'd already proved that a melk was more than my equal. My last-second qualms had slowed me not at all. I'd been beaten because my teeth and claws were inadequate; because I was not a wolf, not a lion, not a Folk.

I crouched below the level of the fat grass, studying them. The Folk studied me. B-beam was at my side, whispering, "We're in no hurry. We've got hours yet. Do you think you can handle a boar-pig?"

"If I could find one I might catch it. But how do I kill it? With my teeth?"

The Folk watched. What did they expect of me?

Suddenly I knew.

"Tell them I'll be in the woods." I pointed. "Just in there. Pick a melk and run it toward me." I turned and moved into the woods, low to the ground. When I looked back everyone was gone.

These trees had to be from the Folk world. They bent to an invisible hurricane. They bent in various directions, because the Mojave environment wasn't giving them the right signals. The trunks had a teardrop-shaped cross section for low wind resistance. Maybe the Folk world was tidally locked, with a wind that came always from one direction. . . .

I dared not go too far for what I needed. The leafy tops of the trees were just in reach, and I plunged my hands in and felt around. The trunk was straight and solid; the branches were no thicker than my big toe, and all leaves. I tried to rip a branch loose anyway. It was too strong, and I didn't have the leverage.

Through the bent trunks I watched melks scattering in panic. But one dashed back and forth, and found black death popping up wherever it looked.

There was fallen stuff on the ground, but no fallen branches. To my right, a glimpse of white—

The melk was running toward the wood.

I ran deeper among the trees. White: bones in a neat pile. Melk bones. I swept a hand through to scatter them. Damn! The leg bones had all been split. What now?

The skull was split too, hanging together by the intertwined horns. I stamped on the horns. They shattered. I picked up a massive half-skull with half a meter of broken horn for a handle.

The melk veered just short of the woods. I sprinted in pursuit. Beyond, B-beam half-stood, his eyes horrified. He shouted, "Rick! No!"

I didn't have time for him. The melk raced away, and nothing popping up in its face was going to stop it now. I was gaining . . . it was fast . . . too damn fast . . . I swung the skull at the flashing hoof, and connected. Again. Throwing it off, slowing it just enough. The half-skull and part-horn made a good bludgeon. I smacked a knee, and it wheeled in rage and caught me across the face and chest with its horns.

I dropped on my back. I got in one grazing blow across the neck as it was turning away, and then it was running and I rolled to my feet and chased it again. There was a feathery feel to my run. My lungs and legs thought I was dying. But the melk shook its head as it ran, and I caught up far enough to swing at its hooves.

This time it didn't turn to attack. Running with something whacking at its feet, it just gradually lost ground. I delivered a two-handed blow to the base of its neck. Swung again and lost my balance and tumbled, caught the roll on my shoulder, had to go back for the skull. Then I ran, floating, recovering lost ground, and suddenly realized that the grass was stirring all around me. I was surrounded by the black shadows of the Folk.

I caught up.

A swing at the head only got the horns. I hammered at the neck, just behind the head. It tumbled, and tried to get to its feet, and I beat it until it fell over. I used the skull like an ax . . . murdering it . . . and suddenly black bodies flowed out of the fat grass and tore at the melk. B-beam got a good grip on the horns and snapped the neck.

I sat down.

He handed me the line: knife, beamer, canteen. He was almost as winded as I was. He whispered, "Damn fool, you weren't—"

"Wrong." I didn't have breath for more. I drank from my canteen, paused to gasp, drank again. Then I turned the beamer on a meaty thigh. The Folk must have been waiting for me to make my choice. They now attacked the forequarters.

I crouched, panting, holding the beamer on the meat until it sizzled, until it smoked, until the smell of it told my belly it was ready.

The heaving of my chest had eased. I handed the knife to B-beam. "Carve us some of that. Eat as much as you can. Courtesy to our hosts."

He did. He gave me a chunk that I needed both hands to hold. It was too hot; I had to juggle it. B-beam said, "You used a weapon."

"I used a club," I said. I bit into the meat. Ecstasy! The famine was over. I hadn't cooked it enough, and so what? I choked down enough to clear my mouth and said, "Humans don't use teeth and claws. The Folk know that. They wanted to see us in action. *My* evolution includes a club."

ONE NIGHT AT THE DRACO TAVERN

T his was the script used for Kathy Sanders's group presentation at the WorldCon Masquerade, Los Angeles, 1984. Steven Barnes played "Rick Schumann." I played "Larry."

Drew and Kathy Sanders generally win major awards in the Masquerades. In 1984 Drew was *running* the Masquerade. Kathy was on her own.

She began making costumes more than a year early. By the time she finished she had duplicated a dozen of the most alien characters from my stories.

I wrote the script. Steven and I recorded the sound background.

The kzin and thrint costumes were *hot*. I had to fan the occupants through their open mouths. The puppeteer must have been worse yet, though it was designed so that Kathy was half out of it until we were called.

I'd seen previous attempts at a Pierson's puppeteer costume. A puppeteer has three legs and two heads. Kathy in her costume had one leg bound up against her chest; heads empty and propped up (they flopped over the first time she tried it); and her arms for the forelegs, on short stilts because human arms aren't long enough. Muscle structure was quilted in, following the Bonnie Dalzell illustration for Ballantine Books, and it looked amazingly lifelike.

She wasn't exactly agile, though.

We won the Master's Award for "Funniest."

ONSTAGE:

Rick Schumann *behind bar. The bar is vertical to the audience.*
Yellow Bugs *around a table.*
Wunderlander *and* Grog *at the bar.*
Qarasht *seated alone, sense cluster retracted.*

ACTION, simultaneously—
Rick *finishes preparing the* Bugs' *order, circles bar and takes them a tray with enough liqueur glasses.*

RICK: Here you are, gentlemen.
Bugs: Queepee? [*sound done with whistle or some such*]

Larry *enters, pulling down zipper or opening buttons and shaking off the cold or the heat (to signal his entry from* outside) *while he looks around. He heads for the* Qarasht.

RICK: It's arak. You'll taste licorice and some other—Wups!

Rick *moves to intercept* Larry.

LARRY: [*to* Qarasht] Hello, I'm—
RICK: I wouldn't talk to the Qarasht if I were you. It doesn't want company.
LARRY: How can you tell?
RICK: It's got its sense cluster retracted.

LARRY: Now, that's my problem. I don't know any of these aliens. Would you be the bartender?

RICK: I own the Draco Tavern. Rick Schumann, at your service. What can I get you?

LARRY: Irish coffee, and a little advice. [*indicates* WUNDERLANDER] Is he human?

MACHINE PEOPLE GIRL *enters, goes to* QARASHT. QARASHT *extrudes sense cluster as she enters.* RICK *moves behind the bar and goes to work, interrupting himself to talk and gesture expansively. He's showing off, as if he owns the customers too.*

    Other aliens are entering—

ENTER:

JINXIAN *and* CRASHLANDER *together*
BELTER (?)

RICK: That's a Wunderlander. Human, but from one of the colonies. Our lady of the beard isn't quite human. She's a Machine People, from the Ringworld. I doubt she can have rishathra with a Qarasht, but she'll probably offer.

LARRY: [*embarrassed*] Hey, can they hear us?

RICK: Naw, they've all got sonic shields. The Jinxian and the Crashlander, they're human too, from Jinx and We Made It. The Belter, the one with the funny haircut, he's from right here in the solar system—

ENTER MOTIE MEDIATOR

ENTER KZIN *and* PUPPETEER, *together*

RICK *continues*:   You'll like the Motie Mediator. Hell, she can interpret for the rest of them. Uh-oh.

LARRY: What's wrong?

RICK: It's all right. It's a Kzin and a Puppeteer, but they don't seem to be fighting.

LARRY: [*indicates* GROG] The, uh, hairy cone at the end of the bar looks interesting . . .

RICK: I don't advise talking to a Grog. She can take over your mind. At least if you run she can't chase you. Heh heh.

LARRY *doesn't get the joke.*

ENTER THRINT

LARRY *turns to look at Thrint.*

RICK *continues*:   Now, that's a rare one. That's a Thrint, what you'd call a Slaver. Stay away—

RICK *interrupts himself to circle the bar, rapidly, carrying* LARRY's *drink.*

LARRY: Why? *(Double take.)* Hey! That's my drink!

RICK *gives the drink to* THRINT, *hastily, and bowing low.*
LARRY *moves to intercept, too slow.*
KZIN *is holding a chair for the* THRINT. JINXIAN *moves a table for him.*

FREEZE FRAME

EXEUNT [*the hale help the clumsier costumes*]

THE HEIGHTS

C*lickety-ponk* came wafting down the magnetic fields above Siberia in the winter of 2041, the fourteenth Chirpsithra liner to visit Earth in twenty-three years. My translator says that *Clickety-ponk* is a pun that means *Weary Light* or *Weary from Mating.* The vast soap bubble of a ship carried forty-one individuals of eight sapient species, five of them unknown to me. All strangers, of course. We'll not see the same liner twice in the same millennium.

One pair, called Warblers, looked like featherless birds. They spent a Tuesday making an aerie just under my ceiling. Tuesday night they sang for us, a concert attended by all the ship's wild variety of crew and passengers. We weren't expected to serve their drinks too, because the Warblers wanted us in the audience, but the *seating!* The Draco Tavern isn't designed as a concert hall.

But the birds were good! They held us rapt. They didn't need microphones, and translators gave us the sense of the lyrics.

Warblers might have been designed by Dick Rutan. A Warbler was the size of a winning jockey, with wings built something like a hawk's under a slick skin of what looked like natural cellophane.

Above a foreshortened beak its head bulged: streamlining sacrificed for a larger brain, porcelain-white eyes that faced straight forward, and stiff canards steered by jaw muscles. They didn't use breathers. They wouldn't touch alcohol. They bought their food in the butcher shops in Mount Forel Town, and warmed it in a microwave oven. Their life-support sigils were almost the same as a human's, tefee tee hatch nex ool, and that was all I needed to keep them happy.

They spent a day on the Internet doing the kind of research a tourist needs. Gail helped with that.

Thursday they were gone.

Monday morning they were back, high overhead in their aerie, not talking to anyone.

Monday evening a man and two children came in.

They had a Midwestern look, lanky and longheaded, with straight black hair. The boy looked about eleven, the girl twelve or thirteen. The children gaped at the aliens. The chirps and some others waved; the children waved back. They were delighted, I judged, but the man was dogged and suspicious. He did not look like a dignitary or anthropologist or university man.

Nobody crosses Siberian tundra to the Draco Tavern in winter just for a drink, and we don't encourage children. I said, "Door, do these have business here?"

The voice of the door, and of the translators and all our other semi-independent systems, said, "This entity spoke of urgent legal business. He asserts that his boy was attacked."

I watched the man approach the bar, holding tight to the hands of the children, who would have hared off among the tables. "Who is he?"

"Z. Wayne Bennett, thirty-two, resides in Ketchum, Idaho, with wife Ida, thirty-five, two children—"

"Pause," I said, because translators at various tables were yammering. "Schumann here."

"Immature life-forms are dangerous, should not be admitted, not likely to be sapient!"

"Who speaks?"

"I am Ambassador-RegentVen! We am not to be endangered!" The system drew blinking green halos around four Lungfish in an over-illuminated vat of water on tractor treads.

All of them? Make that thirty-eight individuals.

I said, "Translator, I'm on it. Tell them that they'll be protected."

"Tell all species?"

"Tell the most timid. Tell Ambassador-Regent Ven and whoever else is complaining. Can you handle it?"

"Yes." I heard hoots and whistles and a low rumble and a skittery rattlesnake sound, alien voices all jabbering at once: the Draco Tavern's translators momentarily linked to perform one service.

Bennett had nearly reached the bar when he suddenly pulled the children against him, pointed straight up, and screamed, "That's them!"

The Lungfish all burrowed straight down into mud. The rest of us all looked up.

The Tavern is built to Chirpsithra design, though humans were the builders and the place is human-friendly. Chirpsithra stand eleven feet tall, and they like head room. Bennett was looking forty feet up to the aerie the birds had built under the ceiling.

Two Warbler faces stared back for a moment, and then one bird launched and tilted into a tight spiral. It wore a thick silver plate with a small rocket pod sticking up on a fin, the base held in place by webbing across its puffer-pigeon chest.

Damage control needed. I eeled around from behind the bar, big smile, hand extended. "I'm Rick Schumann," I said. "You'd be Z. Wayne Bennett?"

He didn't look down, but his hand reached out. "Pleased to meet you, Doctor Schumann. This is Lilly, this is Hammett. Ham was the one attacked. What are you doing about these undead birds?"

"Hi Ham, hi Lilly." I shook their hands. "Attacked?"

The boy grinned. In a sudden motion he peeled off his T-shirt. There were small red marks on both sides of both shoulders, nine marks and a Band-Aid.

Aw shit.

The Warbler dropped lower. He was giving Bennett the creeps. For an instant I saw the Warbler as he did: a cross between a plucked chicken and a bluebellied demon, vicious beak, huge claws built for ripping, the head too human or not human enough. He landed halfway across the main room, on an empty table, and waited.

A child-stealing alien was about the worst publicity I could think of. "I don't see police," I said. "Or reporters."

"You will," Bennett said, "if we don't get this settled. Do I have to worry that my boy got infected with something weird?"

"No, trust me on that." No visitor carries parasites. It's damn few alien bacteria that have an interest . . . though I'm hosting one myself. That one got through by outwitting the medics.

"Here." I fixed a translator to his shirt collar. "Let *me* talk." He nodded once, jaw clenched. I led him and the children to the bird's table.

We had an audience. Even the Lungfish had come out to watch.

The bird watched with unruffled dignity as I settled the Bennetts in chairs. I told it, "I'm Rick Schumann, speaking for—"

"I know you. That one shot my mate."

Bennett glared. I spoke before he could. "Your mate is accused of stealing a child."

"Stealing was not her intent, nor mine. We pick up chosen prey, fly in a circle of designated circumference, and set it down. No harm—"

"Her claws pierced his skin."

"We must acquire gloves. Hammett Bennett, we are sorry for your hurt. Doctor Schumann, this worked out well enough in France when I took prey."

Bennett didn't like *that*, though he held his tongue. I said, "What are your names?"

The bird shrieked musically, twice, then said, "I have been called Langue d'Argent." My translator said, "Silver Tongue."

The United Nations Free Sky (or "Free Spy") Treaty allows satellites to pass over any country at ninety kilometers or above, and any observer may watch it if he can. The Warblers took a lens lander, the smallest of *Clickety-ponk*'s boats, a quarter around the planet and down in Alsace. The boat's stealthing was minimal and the sky, as Silver Tongue described it, was full of hot air balloons that day, but the Warblers would be gone before anyone could react.

What kind of idiots had the Chirps wished upon us this time? "In front of a sky full of witnesses, did you attack a creature that wore clothing?"

"I lifted and carried away a local sapient, a human child whom I had observed with family. These are not mere customs, but lessons hard learned. A creature not sapient can die of the shock or kill itself trying to break free, and herders or conservationists blame us. With a sapient creature we can reason, we can deal.

"The boy Andre Palanque-Delabrouille will verify that we agreed. I told him I had given him a ride; he accepted that. His female guardian screamed that I was an evil genie. When I offered a silver bar, she called me a silver-tongued genie, but she took it."

I said, "Now, I'm still playing catch-up, so give me a sanity check here—"

"We're sane."

"I'll decide that. You saw a child with an adult woman? You swooped out of the sky and picked him up in your claws . . . hands. Carried him how far?"

"Skreek!" (The translator whispered, "Two hundred twenty-three meters.") "In a loop, then back. The game requires we go against the wind. Land, then talk to woman Rosanne Palanque-Delabrouille."

"Have you given thought to everything that *might* have gone wrong?"

"Much thought."

"She was an older adult. In good health? *She* might have died of shock. The boy will be afraid of plucked chickens for the rest of his life. You offered her silver to say she is the boy's guardian? What if she lied?"

"Surname was the same."

"Did she show you identification?" He shrugged; feathers would have ruffled if he had evolved them. "Dammit. You'd have no contract. The news might be breaking on CNN right now. A child attacked by aliens . . . twice now. The Chirpsithra ships could be asked to leave Earth."

"We harm nobody, and the hunt is fair," Silver Tongue said.

Z. Wayne Bennett spoke for the first time. "Don't give me that! Do you think I can't see you're wearing a flying belt?"

Bennett might be more sophisticated than he looked. Then again, Silver Tongue's gear looked very like a Buck Rogers flying belt. Thrashing for an answer to Bennett's accusation, I noticed how many optical organs were pointed our way, and had my first bright idea.

"Z. Wayne, we're being stared at. I don't like it. Do you? Silver Tongue, is there room in your aerie?"

"There is room—"

"*We* can't fly," Z. Wayne said belligerently.

But I had the kids' interest. I said, "There's an elevator."

We'd used it to lift amazing quantities of meat. It was just a flat plate, wide enough for all of us. Z. Wayne's kids pulled him onto it against some resistance. We went up like a dream, with nothing between us and the drop, and unearthly varieties of sapience spread out below us. I was ready to snatch at a child, but Z. Wayne never let go of them.

Silver Tongue's mate awaited our arrival, then backed away to give us room. We stepped out onto spongy wickerwork woven from Siberian vegetation.

Her right side was swollen way out of proportion, a foam plastic pillow outlining a wing bound tight along her torso. The skin of her face was ravaged and smeared with gel, with two pocks in her beak and a patch over one eye.

Her belly was the same sky blue as her mate's. Where his back was a muddle of earth colors, hers was an elaborate scarlet design outlined in silver. I think the silver was tattooed onto a pattern evolved as a secondary sexual characteristic. I've never been sure. I picture him riding the wind high up, camouflaged against predators higher yet while he looked down for the bright flash and pattern of a possible mate. Mated, he would hunt for them both.

Bennett said, forcing himself, "Ma'am, how are you?"

She said, "Healing, thank you, Mr. Bennett. My eye is already replaced. Wing bones are growing in a template. My name is *Sshreekeetht.* How are you, Hammett?"

"Healing too." She had him awed. "Silverback," he said.

"Show her," his father ordered.

The boy took off his shirt. Silverback looked him over, but came no closer. She said, "Z. Wayne Bennett, you must be wonderfully accurate with a shotgun."

"I didn't have the right load. If you'd been closer, you'd be dead."

"You shot me when I was carrying Ham, yet the boy took no harm." She paused to let us all realize how seriously the man had risked his son's life, then said, "No harm except that my hands convulsed when the blast hit me. Of course we must pay extra for his hurt."

"I thought it was more dangerous to leave him in a predator's grip."

She didn't answer. Bennett turned red. He said, "You hunted him wearing a flying belt."

I said, "Z. Wayne, it strikes me that a lift belt is no different from a hunter's gun except that it's not a weapon. Do you hunt?"

He glared.

"If you were strong enough, you'd hunt without the gun. *Tefee tee hatch nex ool* means their world has lighter gravity, that's the *tefee*, with air enough like ours to breath, that's the *tee*."

"Still cheatin'." To the female, "And who gave *you* the right to hunt *my boy*?"

The female said, "Need."

I said, "Oh, come on."

She said, "Doctor Schumann, the hunt triggers our appetite. We need eat only seldom, but we must gorge then. You can testify."

Bennett said, "What?"

"I ported stocks of their food from the market," I told him. "I haven't seen them eat, but I know how much food goes up. At first none, then *lots*."

"If we can't work up hunger during a hunt," she said, "we become malnourished, or we must take noxious medicine."

"Don't we all," I muttered.

"The effect is temporary. We will be lucky to last twenty days. Then, if we cannot hunt, we must endure cold sleep. We had expected to study Earth and mankind for two years."

I had given his children the thrill of a lifetime, then let Bennett confront the entity he'd shot. She had shown him the risk he had taken with his son's life. If Bennett could stay reasonable, couldn't I? But these idiots were throwing it all away, and I was getting angry.

"You don't have a problem," I said. "If you need to hunt, arrange a hunt! I've hunted with the Folk myself! They sold the TV rights and videotaped it!"

"Hunt by arrangement?" She couldn't believe it.

"Live at eleven," Bennett said grimly.

Better take care of Bennett's grievance first. I said, "Mr. Bennett threatens exposure, as is his right. The price of raising a child until he's finished college is around a hundred thousand American dollars, I think."

"Skeep? Price is stunningly high!"

"You might have got a better price by getting his agreement *first*!"

Silver Tongue asked, "What would you do, warn the victim?"

"Sure."

"No," said Silverback.

"The thing is," Bennett said doggedly, "my wife talked me into coming here first. She's walking today because her spine got fixed by some alien technique I can't spell or pronounce. I'm asking because you might . . . *might* have a rational answer. What gave you the right to attack my son?"

"We must buy that."

"After stealing it!"

Silverback said, "We hoped for two years on Earth, continue on the next liner. If Earth cannot feed us, we must endure cold sleep beginning tomorrow! Feeding aliens, isn't that your business, Rick?" She examined me hopefully; gave up and turned to Ham. "But you are harmed, debt must be paid. Skreee?"

Her mate said, "Price is ridiculous in the up direction."

Ham said, "I'm all right."

I *wanted* the price to sting a little. I said to the birds, "Your sense of proportion is way off. What if you did catch an orphan? There wouldn't *be* anyone to deal with."

"An orphan would be the business of local government," Silver Tongue said.

"Were you ready to ask the French government to *name their price*?" *Sacre bleu,* I thought.

"Is France rapacious?"

"No, it's *governments* that are rapacious . . . and lawyers. You've attacked Ham in the United States of America, where lawyers are thicker than anywhere on Earth!" I had my second bright notion. "You try that again, you'll be lucky not to lose your place aboard *Clickety-ponk* to some small boy with stars in his eyes and a smart-mouthed lawyer." *That* should push some buttons.

Ham stared at me. Then he pulled at his father's sleeve. "Dad?"

Silver Tongue said, "You exaggerate for effect. I offer two bars silver, two pounds each."

Ham's eyes weren't really glowing, and no alien could read so subtle a signal. But Ham and his father were trying to interrupt each other, and suddenly Z. Wayne bellowed, "You would never see me or your mother again! Nor Lilly either! Lilly, talk to him! Silver Tongue, am I right? These ships go slower than light! Even if he caught a ride back from some other star, it could be a hundred years, or a thousand!"

The boy said, "But an *interstellar*—"

Silverback noticed what was going on. "Major decision, give up the past, adjust to far-away unknown future, as we have. Circle the galaxy or stop off at own risk. Up to a hundred thousand years before return. Wait until older, Hammett. Mister Bennett, we accept price to teach Ham through college as determined through the Internet, pay in United States dollars, twenty percent finder fee for rapacious bartender—"

"Hold up," said Z. Wayne.

"—Escrow account for you and Hammett until Hammett attains age of presumed wisdom, if you will sign now."

"There's nothing wrong with the price," Z. Wayne said. "No, dammit, Ham, we will not sue to get you a ticket on an interstellar liner! Silverback, I want some assurance that there will be no further hunting of children."

"We would have to leave Earth early," she said.

"You can't prey on children. No matter what you pay, who you pay, you still can't do that."

The birds were silent. Z. Wayne looked at me.

"I have a notion," I said.

Five months later I took my niece and her children to the Park.

They'd raised the price of tickets by 60 percent. The crowding was fierce. Marilyn was shocked.

"Relax," I told her. "This is Draco Tavern's treat, every dollar of it."

"But why do *they* pay that much? Most children aren't even wearing the hats! Those that are . . . four a day? Out of hundreds!"

"Under two hundred." We'd picked a Wednesday.

The young man wouldn't give Wayne and Becky hats unless Marilyn and I signed contracts as their guardians. Despite four children tugging at us, I took a couple of minutes to examine the contract. I wanted to be sure no sneaky little weasel clauses had crept in since we wrote it.

A lot of parents were changing their minds after they read it. I signed.

"Ricky, *is* this safe?"

"Sure. Jael? Alvin? Han?" Had they changed their minds?

They made their intent clear, and Marilyn signed, and the kids put on the hats. Han asked, "Can I keep it?"

"It's a loaner," Marilyn said.

I said, "You can buy it when you leave."

Scattered through a crowd of a thousand were less than a hundred hats, all on children between five and ten, all flame orange with a wide brim for protection against the sun and against looking up. Children with and children without orange hats all looked up anyway as they entered the Park. We found cloudless blue sky, and the new tower.

"Where are they?" Denise demanded.

I shook my head. "The tower's theirs. They come when they want. Only the top, of course." Most of the tower was the Beanstalk Fall, with much too long a waiting line. "Hey, Dolphin Ride!"

A prey who welcomes us is not acceptable!" Silverback kept repeating herself. She was *sure* I didn't understand.

"First remember what you're avoiding," I told her. "Two years in cold sleep, then off into the starscape. Even doing it my way, you'll lose time while the lawyers argue."

"No!"

"Bet on six months, plus or minus. You can't have everything. What you *can* have," I said, "is prey that don't know you're coming."

"Nonsense! They sign contracts!"

"Look again. The Park gets seven hundred people on a weekday, three times that on weekends. Half of those are kids," exaggerating a little. "You pick two in a day. Four if you can stand it. It's less than a hundred to one that any kid gets picked.

"A lot of them, kids and parents, will spend the whole time looking up." Memo: Be *damn* sure the Park makes dark glasses available! "You don't pick those. Ignore them. Others will forget you're there. You're not on a schedule. It's an *amusement park.* They'll be *distracted.*"

Z. Wayne had been working with a Palm Pilot. "Can you really get away with this? You're selling very little. Pot odds are of any kid being carried one and a half feet by two-point-two pounds of bird."

"Most of them won't wear the hats! Z. Wayne, they'll pay extra to see *some other kid* carried off. Most of the kids *with* hats won't get more than that."

"They'll never buy it," said Bennett.

"Shall I put out offers?"

"Try it," said Bennett, and "One may ask," said Silverback, and "Scraww!" said Silver Tongue. So I put in calls to Disney, Knott's, Six Flags. . . .

Music from the sky.

We all looked up. The birds were there, black against the sun, singing their hearts out. They wheeled and sang for at least ten minutes above the endless line for the Beanstalk Fall, then glided behind the tower in a roar of applause.

I faced forward again. The kids were tired of waiting.

Screams. I looked around.

The birds had circled behind the tower, already diving, picking up serious speed. They fell straight toward us. Silverback pulled up and rolled, showing her silver-and-scarlet design, but Silver Tongue swerved and swooped and dropped on an eight-year-old girl.

For an instant I wished fiercely that Disney World had bid. All that empty land for the birds! And they could have been wearing yellow Mickey Mouse hands! But Disney hadn't even got in a bid; their lawyers were too timid. Silver Tongue's claw tips were sheathed in blue, the color of his belly, and the girl never saw them until they closed on her. We heard her scree-hee-hee-heeming, fear and laughter as she rose.

THE WISDOM OF
DEMONS

With the midnight sun behind him, he entered the Draco Tavern as a fire-edged black silhouette. Even so, I knew him.

I watched him approach the bar. His walk was wobbly and he was being careful of his balance, like a karate master just out of the hospital. He'd been drinking last night . . . wait, now, it wasn't him at all.

Then he wrestled himself onto a stool and adjusted the height, and I knew him again. "Webber, wasn't it? Last night."

A goofy, twisted grin. It wasn't Webber. "Yes! Alan Webber, anthropologist. Give me water. Flavored water."

"I've got some carbonated fruit flavors—"

"Good!"

I ducked back into storage.

The Draco Tavern serves every species that travels with the Chirpsithra interstellar liners. Our storage space has to be huge, but stuff for human consumption is stacked along one short wall. I picked him a cranberry soda, then took a moment to get my nerve back.

Last night he'd called himself a xenosociologist. His speech, his walk, his look were all different. There weren't many aliens in the bar last night, and two or three times as many humans. Webber had started talking to a Gligstith(click)optok.

What I know about the Glig is privileged. I'd given Webber no more warning than what we tell everybody. Nobody gets near Mount Forel, Siberia, without hearing it a dozen times: *These are ETIs, interstellar travelers. Gangrene is your first cousin compared to these entities. They don't think like you do.* . . .

They'd gone to a table and turned on a privacy shield.

The Glig showed him wonders. I've seen their toys, technology beyond anything we've been able to borrow or copy, and weird little plants and animals. They talked half the night. At two in the morning, with the low July sun coming around from behind Mount Forel, Webber and the Glig went off toward the lander.

And here he was again, but changed.

I've run the Draco Tavern for years. From time to time I see the usual strangeness edging over into horror or madness. I deal with it. Whatever was wrong here, if I complained to any Chirpsithra she would relay it to the captain. And I had the stun.

So what was I afraid of?

I showed him the bottle. "This is cranberry. Ice?"

"Good idea!"

"Splash of dark rum on top?"

"Try it."

He'd ordered scotch and soda last night. Maybe he'd get loquacious. I served him and watched him taste. He twitched, startled at the bite of the rum.

"You were with a Glig last night. With," I remembered, "Preez Thporshkil."

"Yes. Thporshkil offered . . . Ow."

"Ow?"

"I bit my lip," he said. Some customers wear a slack and gaping grin the whole time they're in here, like everything they see is new and different. *He* wore that grin as if sketched in by a drunken artist with a shaky hand. "Offered me a wish."

I asked, "A wish? Like a genie or a devil?"

His face went slack. Then, "Yes, like a genie, but there must be many wishes. . . . you say *Glig*? Many wishes a *Glig* can't grant. Thporshkil is studying the human kind. It wanted to see what I would ask and what I would do with it. What would you wish for, Rick?"

Alan Webber had asked me that question last night. I should have guessed what was going on.

I said, "Make me healthy."

He laughed oddly. "Not a good choice!"

"Glig are masters of biology."

"We, they, Glig love the life sciences. They wish to learn more of human chemistry . . . plumbing . . . interior interactions . . . array of nerve interactions. The corpus callosum that connects the two halves of your brain, why is it so narrow?"

"Beats me. I think it's why some of us talk to ourselves. We have to get signals from one side of the brain to the other."

"Yes, of course! But Thporshkil would use the opportunity to learn, to experiment. Once he began work on you, you would be left in too terrible a state ever to say, 'Stop!' until Thporshkil had repaired all of its mistakes. But . . . no, wait . . . Rick, in the end you would be healthy to the limit of Thporshkil's skill. Ow." He pronounced the Glig's name better than I did, but it had him biting his lip over and over. "You would want the chaotic damage of many years repaired? Your life extended? Nose and brow and ears reshaped?"

"Hey!"

"In time Thporshkil could learn to do all that. Rick, I can arrange it."

Webber hadn't called me *Rick*. Last night he'd called me *Dr. Schumann*. But the Gligstith(click)optok couldn't say *Schumann*.

"Webber," I said, though I had become sure that this wasn't Webber, "what did you ask for?" I was examining him for seams and flaps, not trying to hide it much. I thought he might be a copy, some kind of android, and he'd need access hatches.

He said, "I wished for Thporshkil's wisdom."

"Just that?"

"Yes. If you ask a . . . demon? for health, it must make you healthy to its own limit of skill, if you don't add limits by using modifiers. Adjectives. But that is your wish. I wanted the wisdom of an interstellar traveler."

Again I felt my bloodstream icing up. I said, "That was a bad wish. Your brain might not be big enough. Or you could end up knowing things meant for Glig, not for humans. They wouldn't go to a toilet the same way, or reproduce—"

"No!" That wild laugh again.

I said, "Glig eat human meat, did you know that?"

"I didn't know it last night. Rick, they don't kill to get it! They're only curious. They clone human organs for the markets. As for brains, Glig and human nervous systems are vastly capacious. The limit is not the number of brain cells, but the number of possible connections. Only a storage algorithm is needed. Thporshkil downloaded my mind, copied itself, wrote a merge program, merged us and wrote it all back into my brain. Here I am. When I come back here in two hundred days, Thporshkil too will have its wish. It will learn what I can learn of what it is to be a man."

"Wisdom," I said. "Suppose you'd wished for knowledge?"

"Thporshkil might have given me knowledge. Light-threads from his library and a viewer to string them." Webber's strange pronunciation was improving. "But wisdom is knowledge and the skill to use what you know. I wanted both."

"Did you get what you wanted?"

"Yes!"

"This change, is it permanent?"

"You mean to ask if my new knowledge can be taken away from me."

"Filtered out," I suggested, "leaving what you were." Was there a way to rescue last night's Alan Webber?

He asked, "Rick, can you make a machine to separate the components of a milkshake?"

"I might."

"But it would be elaborate and expensive and hard to market," he said, "and too massive to ride aboard a chirps liner."

"But are you Alan Webber? Or did he die last night? It's pretty clear that you're also Thporshkil the Gligstith(click)optok."

I had my hand near the stun, but he hadn't even lost the goofy grin. "I'm here. I may answer for either of us, Thporshkil or Alan. Do you think I was cheated?" Webber laughed. "I have wisdom now!"

"You sure as hell didn't last night. Did you ever make a sillier wish in your life?"

"Rick, most animals seek homeostasis, but interstellar travelers are different. We are not like those who stay home. We seek change. The man I was last night wanted to change himself. He has his wish. I do not have a complaint. Do you? You know who to speak to."

He walked out, perfectly in balance and almost strutting. I thought it over, and in the end I did nothing.

SMUT TALK

The Draco Tavern isn't just a pub. It's how humanity interacts with at least twenty-eight sapient species throughout the galaxy. Somewhere among these trillions of alien minds are the answers to all of the universal questions.

So it's worth the expense, but costs are high. Keeping supplies in hand grows more difficult every time a new species appears. Siberian weather tears the Draco Tavern down as fast as we can rebuild it.

When a year passed without a Chirpsithra ship, we were glad of the respite. The Tavern got some repairs. I got several months of vacation in Wyoming and Tahiti. Then that tremendous Chirpsithra soap bubble drifted inward from near the Moon, and landers flowed down along the Earth's magnetic lines to Mount Forel in Siberia.

For four days and nights the Draco Tavern was very busy.

On the fifth morning, way too early, one hundred and twenty-four individuals of ten species boarded the landers and were gone.

The next day Gail and Herman called in sick. I didn't get in until midafternoon, alone on duty and fighting a dull headache.

We weren't crowded. The security programs had let the few customers in and powered up various life-support systems. The few who didn't mind staying another year or two were all gathered around our biggest table. Eight individuals, five . . . make it four species including a woman.

I'd never seen her before. She was dressed in a short-skirted Italian or American business suit. Late twenties. Olive Arabic features. Nose like a blade, eyes like a hawk. I thought she was trying to look professionally severe. She was stunning.

The average citizen never reaches the Draco Tavern. To get here this woman must have been passed by her own government, then by the current UN psychiatric programs, Free Siberia, and several other political entities. She'd be some variety of biologist. It's the most common credential.

Old habit pulled my eyes away. The way I was feeling, I wasn't exactly on the make, and I didn't need to wonder what a human would eat, drink, or breathe. Tee tee hatch nex ool, her Chirpsithra life-support code was the same as mine. My concern was with the aliens.

I recognized the contours of a lone Wahartht from news coverage. They're hexapods with six greatly exaggerated hands, from a world that must be all winds. They'd gone up Kilimanjaro in competition with an Olympic climbing team. Travelers are supposed to be all male. This one had faced a high-backed chair around and was clinging to the back, looking quite comfortable. He was wearing a breather.

The three Folk had been living in the Kalahari, hunting with the natives. They looked lean and hungry. That was good. When they look like Cujo escaped from Belsen with his head on upside down, then they're mean and ravenous and not good bar company.

Gray Mourners were new to Earth. They're spidery creatures, with narrow torsos and ten long limbs that require lots of room, and big heads that are mostly mouth. I'd taken them for two species; the sexual disparity was that great. Two males and a female, if the little ones were males, if that protrusion was what I thought it was.

The gathering of species all seemed to be getting along. You do have to watch that.

As I stepped into the privacy bubble the woman was saying, "Men mate with anything—" and then she sensed me there and turned, flushing.

"Welcome," I said, letting the translator program handle details of formality. "Whatever you need for comfort, we may conceivably have it. Ask me. Folk, I know your need."

One of the Folk (I'd hunted with these, and *still* never learned to tell their gender) said, "Greeting, Rick. You will join us? We would drink bouillon or glacier water. We know you don't keep live prey."

I grinned and said, "Whatever you see may be a customer." I turned to the woman.

She said, "I'm Jehaneh Miller."

"I'm Rick Schumann. I run this place. Miller?"

"My mother was American." So was her accent. Briskly she continued, "We were talking about sex. I was saying that men make billions of sperm, women make scores of eggs. Men mate with anything, women are choosy." She spoke as if in challenge, but she was definitely blushing.

"I follow. There's more to be said on *that* topic. What are you drinking?"

"Screwdriver, light."

"Like hers," the Waharht said. Aliens rarely order alcoholic drinks twice, but some just have to try it.

The female Gray Mourner asked, "Did our supplies arrive?"

They had. I went back to the bar.

Beef bouillon and glacier water for the Folk. Screwdrivers, light, for the woman and the Wahartht, but first I checked my database to be sure a Wahartht could digest orange juice. I made one for myself, for the raspy throat.

The Gray Mourners were eating stuff that I'd never seen until that afternoon, an orange mash that arrived frozen. Tang sherbet?

I assembled it all quickly. I wanted to hear what they were saying. A great many aliens had left Earth very suddenly, and I hoped for a hint as to why.

And . . . given the conversational bent, I might learn something of Jehaneh Miller.

As I set down the drinks the Wahartht was saying, "Our child bearers cannot leave their forests, cannot bear change of smells and shading and diet, nor free fall nor biorhythm upset. We can never possess much of our own planet, let alone others. The females send us forth and wait for us to bring back stories."

A Folk said, "You are all male. Do you live without sex?"

The Wahartht jumped; he tapped his translator. "'Survive without impregnation activity.' Was that accurately your question?"

"Yes."

"Without scent and sonic cues, we never miss it."

Jehaneh nodded and said to me, "Most life-forms, the mating action is wired in." To the Wahartht, "Does that hold for sapient species too?"

The Wahartht said, "Impregnation is reflex to us. Our minds almost do not participate. Away from our females, we take a tranquilizing biochemical to inhibit a sometime suicidal rage."

I said, "I'm not surprised."

"But what should I miss?"

A Gray Mourner male cried out, "To return from orgasmic joy and be still alive!"

The other male chimed in. "Yes, Wajee! It always feels like we're getting away with something." I grinned because I agreed, but he was saying, "We think this began our civilization. Species like ours, female eats male just after take his generative pellet."

I think I flinched. The woman Jehaneh didn't. She cogitated, then asked, "What if you shove a beefsteak in her mouth?"

They're not insects, I wanted to say. *Aliens!* But nobody took offense. All three Gray Mourners chittered in, I assumed, laughter.

Wajee said, "Easy to say! No male can think of such a thing when giving generative pellet. Like design and build a parachute while riding hurricane! But what if two males? One male have sex. The other male, he put turkey in Sfillirrath's mouth."

Jehaneh jumped. "A whole turkey?"

The female smiled widely. Yike! Her jaw hinges disjointed like a snake's. Sfillirrath was twice the mass of either male, and her smile could have engulfed my head and shoulders too.

She said, "On Earth, a turkey or dog will serve. Taste wrong, even if feed spices to the animal, but size is right. Size of Wajee's head, or Shkatht's head. See you the advantage? Can have sex twice with the same male! Get better with practice, yes, Shkatht?"

"Almost got it right," Shkatht said complacently. "Next time for sure."

Wajee said, "Got to get one part right every time."

They chittered laughter. Wajee said, "Accident can happen. Turkey can escape. Resting male can be distracted, or remember old offense and not move quick."

Sfillirrath said, "But see anti-advantage? Males don't die. Too many males. Soon every female must have many mates, or else rogue males tear down cities."

Wajee said, "Mating frequency rises too. Too many mouths. Must invent herding."

"Herd, then tend crop to feed herd. Then cities and factories. Then barrier bag over placer tube," Sfillirrath said, "so don't make a clutch of infants every curse time! Now we mate without mating, but need cities to support factories to make barrier bags, laws and lawmakers to enforce use. Control air and water flow, cycle waste, spacecraft to moons for raw resources, first contact with Chirpsithra, beg ride to see the universe and here are we. All for a perversion of nature."

Jehaneh asked the Folk, "How do you keep your numbers in bounds?"

"Breed more dangerous prey," one answered.

The female Gray Mourner asked, "How do humans pervert sex practice?"

I asked the woman, "Shall I take this?" She gestured, *Go.*

I suppose I shaded the truth a bit toward what she might want to hear. "What Jehaneh said isn't all true. Most of us don't mate with anything but adults of the other gender. Most men *know* that most women want one mate. Most women *know* that any man can be seduced. We make bargains and promises and contracts. We compromise. To go against human nature is the most human thing a human being can do."

The Folk laughed. Jehaneh was watching me. I said, "We're a young species. In an older species the sexual reflexes would be hardwired." I wasn't sure that would translate, but none of the devices paused. Any space traveler uses computers. "But with us, sex involves the mind. We're versatile."

"We have barrier bags too," Jehaneh said. A moment's eye contact—*Condoms, of course, and had I caught the reference?* I flashed a smirk.

Still, I wouldn't be needing a barrier bag tonight. The rasp at the back of my throat told me that I'd be snuffling and coughing and gender free. I was lucky it had held off this long.

A Folk asked, "How are you versatile? Male with male? With sexual immature? Outside species?"

Sfillirrath asked, "Triads?"

"You've been reading the tabloids," I guessed.

Jehaneh said primly, "All of that has been known to happen. We discourage it."

"There are legends," I said. "Old stories that weren't written down until centuries after they were made. Mermaids were half woman, half sea life—"

"And mermen," she said.

"Jehaneh, those are modern," I said. "When sailors were all men, mermaids were all women with fish tails and wonderful voices."

Jehaneh asked, "Are you an anthropologist, Rick?"

"Sure."

"What discipline? What's your education?"

I'd been lecturing on her turf. My head throbbed. It does that sometimes when I'm challenged, but this was the day's low-level headache lurching into high gear. I must have caught what Gail and Herman had.

I reeled off some of my credits. "If you think about it, I need *every* life science to run this place, and e-mail addresses for everyone in the Science Fiction Writers of America. If you're an anthropologist, you might consider working here for a year or so. We rotate fairly frequently, and both my steadies are out at the moment—"

"No, I'm a bacteriologist."

Bacteriologist? How was I going to get closer to a bacteriologist? I was trying to plan for the long range . . . and the aliens weren't following this at all.

I said, "We humans, we do seem wired up to mate with strangers, outside the tribe. At least in fiction, yeah, Jehaneh, we'd mate with anything. Fairies were powerful aliens, nearly human, not very well described. Humans with goat horns or animal heads, goat legs, fish tails, wings. Some were *that* tall," hands eight inches apart, "others the size of mountains. Spirits in trees and pools of water, angels and devils and gods from various myths and religions, they all mated with human beings in some stories. I'm telling you what's buried in our instincts. We don't always act on our instincts." I realized I was rambling.

"Rick, do you have any visual aids about?"

I gaped. Jehaneh's smile seemed innocent, but the question was impish.

"I don't think so." A raunchy thought crossed my mind. "Do a demonstration?"

"I don't think you'll be up for that," Jehaneh said.

"No, not tonight . . . flu."

She shook her head. "Invader. I came here to keep it confined."

Confined. Invader. Bacteriologist. A murky truth congealed: I didn't have the flu. Some alien disease had come with the Chirp-sithra ship. I started to say something to Jehaneh, tried to stop myself, and found my thoughts running away like water.

The Wahartht leapt to the table, then the wall. He scuttled toward an upper window, his thirty-six fingers finding purchase where there was none. Jehaneh reached into her purse.

In that moment's distraction I turned to run . . . wondered what I was doing . . . and every muscle locked in terror. Not even my scream could get out. The Goddamned flu was thinking with my brain!

Jehaneh aimed her purse. The Wahartht fell, stunned. I saw it all from the corner of my eye. I couldn't turn my head to watch.

Jehaneh reached forward and turned off my translator. She spoke into her own. "Bring them in."

I couldn't lift my arms. Escape was impossible: the host was fighting me. My head was beating like a big drum.

Sfillirrath's long, fragile arms set a cap of metal mesh on my head. She spoke into her own translator. It was a Chirp make, crudely rewired. I heard, but not with my ears and not in any language of Earth, ~For your life, you must speak.~

I chose not to answer.

Two armored men took charge of the Waharht. One took his breather and dropped it in a bag and sealed it, and set another on his face.

Gail and Herman came in. They bent above me, looking worried. Gail said, "Rick? You're very sick. We were too, but they cured us—"

"Don't agree to anything!" Herman said fiercely. "Not unless you want to make medical history!"

Sfillirrath spoke. ~See you these humans. You took them for hosts some days ago, you and your Waharht pawn. Your colonies bred too fast for their health. In another day they would have killed them, but human defenders acted first. Most of your colonies on the ship are dead too. How did you reward a Waharht, to make him betray so many?~

I said, not with my voice, ~Simulate mating. The drug he takes to tranquilize depression does not leave him alert and happy. I do.~

~And what fool would assume that sapient beings cannot fight bacterial invasion? It may be you are not truly sapient.~

Stung, I answered, ~Am a star-traveling species. Hold many worlds.~

~Your number in the host is?~

~Currently ten to the ninth operators, one entity. Operators are not sapient, not *me*.~

~Breed to ten times as many, entity becomes smarter?~

~Only a little.~

~But too many for host. Rick Schumann would die. Kill host, is that intelligent?~

The voice in my mind asked, ~Fool, do you expect intelligence to stop an entity from breeding?~ I thought that was a funny remark, so I added, "Ask any elected official." My voice was an inaudible whisper.

Gail said, "Rick, the Chirp liner is still near the Moon. The point was to get all the tourists into closed cycle life support and not start a panic on Earth. There's a sapient microscopic life-form loose. This rogue Wahartht has been leaning over our drinks with his breather on, distributing the bacterium as a powder, in encysted form. Normally it spreads as a, um, a social disease. Under proper circumstances it is a civilized entity, not especially trustworthy but it can be held to contracts. But as a disease it could ravage the Earth."

I could barely blink.

"We can make treaties with sapient clusters of the bacterium. That's you. Some species can't tolerate it at all, and some clusters won't negotiate. Some aliens won't volunteer as carriers, either. Herman and me, we would have. Hell, we're grad students! But there wasn't time. They rushed us to the Medical facility and shot us full of sulfa drugs."

Sfillirrath had gone on talking. ~There is a chemical approach to halt your cell division. Antibiotics would kill you entirely, as they have killed your other colonies. Which will you have?~

I felt terror from both sides of my mind. ~If my operators do not fission, still they die. When the numbers drop enough, I am gone. You would make me mortal!~

~Give you empathy with your host.~

~Monster, pervert! What would you know of empathy? I will accept the contraceptive.~

~You must buy it,~ Sfillirrath said coolly. ~This first dose is our gift.~ "Jehaneh, give him the first shot." ~Two boosters to come, else the sulfa drugs. We will discuss terms.~

Jehaneh pulled down my belt and pushed a hypodermic needle into the glutial muscle. I barely felt the sting.

I listened to Sfillirrath's terms, and agreed to them. They included measures for the health of my host. My host was to be treated for arthritis, cholesterol buildup, distorted eyesight, a knee injury, flawed teeth. I was not to make colonies without permission of a willing host. Jehaneh offered herself as a host, under rigidly defined conditions, and I agreed to those. Xenologists of many species would interview me periodically.

I was feeling more lucid. When I could stand up, they escorted me off to the Medical facility.

Morning. I lay on a flat plate with a sensor array above me. I'd never seen the Draco Tavern Medical facility from this viewpoint.

I felt wonderful. Rolled out of bed and did a handstand, something I hadn't done in some time.

Jehaneh caught me at it. "I'm glad to see you're up to exercise," she said. "What do you remember?"

"First flu, then an invasion, now it's an embassy. Jehaneh, I can hear it. It's thinking with my brain. I think it's got the hots for you, but that could be just me."

"We agreed that I'll take a colony from you. Remember?"

"No. That sounds risky! Jehaneh, it would be like being an ambassador to, well, Iraq."

"They do build embassies in Iraq," she said, "and this is a star-traveling intelligence. What might I learn?"

"Huh. Your choice. And it'll fix . . ." I was remembering more of the negotiations. "I thought I was in pretty good health, but it wants to do a lot of fixing. To show how useful it can be. You're the brain it really wants."

"Do you remember that it's a sexually transmitted, um, entity?"

I did. I leered.

We talked much as we had last night, but on a more personal level. Ultimately she asked, "We've both had the usual blood tests, yes? Our guest would fix that anyway. Do you have room for me here? Just until I can get infected." She didn't like that word. "Colonized," she said.

"Positively. Maybe I can talk you into staying longer? My bed has one or two unearthly entertainment features. And if a hundred breeds of alien are going to be interviewing your guest, well, the Draco Tavern has the best communication and life-support systems on Earth."

She smiled. "We'll see."

Ssoroghod's People

A week after the first Chirpsithra liner arrived, a second ship winkled out of interstellar space. It paused to exchange courtesies with the ship now hovering alongside the Moon, then pulled up next to it.

It was as big as the liner whose passengers had filled the Draco Tavern for seven nights now. We'd never had two of these in dock. The media were going nuts, of course. I worried about all these extra aliens. How was I going to fit them in?

The Draco Tavern's ceilings are high enough for bird analogues to fly. I could set some tables floating. . . .

When a handful of Chirpsithra crew came in, I took the opportunity to ask. "How many more tables am I going to need?"

"One," said a ship's officer. "One occupant."

"How big?" The Chirpsithra deal with entities bigger than a blue whale.

"Ssoroghod is one of us, a Chirpsithra. Sss," as she touched the sparker with her fingertips. "She flies a long-term habitat and environment-shaping system. Much cargo space," she said.

Next day a ship's boat drifted down the magnetic lines to

Mount Forel. Presently an inflated sphere rolled across the hard November tundra, attached itself to one of the Tavern's airlocks, and deflated to let in a Chirpsithra.

The newcomer made for the bar, passing six crew from the first ship. They all look alike, or pretty close, but I noticed differences. The newcomer's decorative crest (and news and entertainment set) was in a very different style. Her salmon armor differed just a bit, graying at the edges of the plates. She was old.

One spoke to her. She chose not to hear, walked regally past, and was at the bar. To me she said, "Dispenser, a sparker."

I had one ready. The chirps only have, or only show, this one sin.

She put her thumbs on the sparker and kept them there. I'd never seen a Chirp do that. Her antennae were trembling. She was getting too much of a charge.

She let go. Her posture shifted, lolling. She said, "Dispenser, sparkers for my companions at table zith-mm. Tell them to remember—" She rattled off numbers in her own language.

I took sparkers to the chirps' table. Props. They already had theirs. I said, "A gift from the citizen at the bar. She sent you a message." My translator also records. I ran it back to the right time and played it for them.

One said, "A location."

"That was *her* station," another said. "Whee-Nisht variants one through four. Ssoroghod had them in her charge. She sent us sparkers?"

"Memorial," said a third. "They must be extinct."

"She will not talk to us. Ssoroghod was always unsocial."

I asked, "Can you tell me what's wrong with her?"

They looked at each other. I thought they wouldn't answer, but one said, "She may choose suicide."

"How would I stop that?"

"Why would you?"

Death has happened in the Draco Tavern. Once it was a memorial service with the main guest alive until halfway through. Both times, the individuals kept it neat. I still don't like it.

One said, "She spoke to you. Rick Schumann, let her talk. She may persuade herself to live."

Humans use the bar chairs when they need to talk to the bartender. Most of the chirps' clients need a tailored environment; they go to the tables, which can be enclosed. The bar doesn't get much action from aliens. Chirps themselves can breath Earth's air; it's the lighting that gets to them.

At the bar tonight there was only Ssoroghod, eleven feet tall though she weighed no more than I did, armored in red exoskeletal plates fading to gray at the edges, and some prosthetic gear. I told her, "The tables might have lighting more to your taste."

"I do not want the company of my kind. This bluer light, I endured it for—" She gave a number. My translator said, "—One million thirty thousand years."

Mistranslation? I said, "That's a long time."

Nothing.

"What were you doing?"

"Watching."

I guessed: "Watching the Whee-Nisht? Variants one through four?"

She said, "Variants two and three made pact, intermated, merged, crowded out the others. They were competing for too limited an environment. Variants one and four died out."

"Why were you watching them?"

For a minute I thought she wouldn't answer. Should I leave her alone, or risk driving her away? Then she said, "We found a species on the verge of sapience.

"The Whee-Nisht held a limited environment, a sandy coastline along the eastern shore of the megacontinent. Their metabolism was based on silicon dioxide. They adapted too well to the local diet, gravity, lighting, salinity of water, local symbiotes. They would never conquer any large part of their own world, let alone go among the stars. I could study them and still stay out of their way. This was the basis on which I was given permission to watch them evolve.

"I watched them grow along the Fertile Band. I was pleased when they tamed other life-forms and bred them for desired traits. Though sworn not to interfere with their development, I did divert a meteoroid impact that would have altered local coastlines. They might have gone extinct." She touched the sparker, just brushed it. "But they might have evolved flexibility. I cannot know. Mistake or no, I shifted the killer rock.

"Their numbers then grew overgreat. I wondered if I must act again, but they adapted, developed a yeast for contraception. It was their first clear act to change themselves."

"What went wrong?"

She focused on me. I had the impression that she was only now seeing me.

"Dispenser . . . Rick Schumann . . . do you use something like sparkers? A jolt to change your viewpoint?"

I said my kind used alcohol. At her invitation I made myself an Irish coffee. I sipped meagerly. Being drunk might be bad.

She said, "Whee-Nisht have completed a cycle, a pattern. They are extinct. Does that always mean something has gone wrong?"

"It would to me," I said.

Her head nodded above me. Thumbs brushed the sparker. Then, "I saw no reason to interfere when they altered other life-forms. They made and shaped and reshaped foodstuffs, beasts of burden, guard beasts. Yeast analogues became flavoring for food,

medicines, perception-altering substances. Plants were bred taller
and stronger, to improve structure for their housing, then water-
going vessels to explore beyond their domain. When they began
using similar techniques to shape themselves, I saw startling im-
plications.

"I acted at once," she said. "I set a terraforming project in motion on a large island just beyond their horizon. My intent was to
build an environment the match for their own, without affecting
theirs. Guiding weather patterns required exquisite care. When I
finished, there was an island that might house the Whee-Nisht,
and a sandy peninsula pointing straight at it.

"Now I—"

I asked, "Why?"

She focused on me. "They had shaped the contraceptive
yeast. Now they began to breed their offspring and siblings and
dependents to make patterns, to conserve wealth and power rela-
tions and to shape offspring more to their liking. Crimes were
defined and criminals were subject to mental reshaping. I asked
myself, how would they otherwise tamper with their selves? One
mistake would drive them extinct. It has happened to other
species, over and over. Dispenser, what is it your kind uses for
reproductive code?"

"Deoxyribonucleic acid," I said.

"The Whee-Nisht used a different code, being silicon oxide
based, but no matter. I was in a race for their lives. By the time
they learned how to manipulate their own genetics, I was done.
The ocean currents were bringing them bubble plants, telling
them of a second habitat beyond the water. They built exploring
vehicles, and they found it."

"Ships?"

"Great translucent tubes, grown as plants, that rolled along
sand or waves. They reached my second land and named it Anti-
home. I watched them build a base and explore from there.

I waited for them to enlarge it. My intent was that they would build a city. Nearby they could do their biological experiments, where any mistake could be confined."

She touched the sparkers again, held too long. I waited.

She asked, "Do you understand why this self-tampering kills so many species? It is so easy, so cheap. Knowledge of genetic code is not needed. What you like, breeds. What you don't like, you uproot. Planned breeding may take generations, but not wealth. It is exploration that eats wealth. Your kind could tamper with yourselves for a million years for the cost of putting a city on your Moon, using your own primitive techniques.

"But you, you have the option! Most species could not travel between worlds. It would kill them. The Whee-Nisht could barely cross a channel, half dead of motion sickness and running like thieves along their rolling ship, and reach an island prepared for them.

"And they threw it away.

"They explored, and came home, and stopped. They abandoned their bases, their tools, everything.

"Their laboratories shaped a cure for a genetic disorder out of a yeast variant. They did not guess that it would prevent the next generation from breeding. They did not guess that it would spread through their spiracle-analogues and infect all. I watched them grow old and die, and this time I did not interfere."

I asked, "Did you ask advice from other . . . xenoanthropologists? Others of your profession?" Amateur godlings? But a million years of practice does not leave an amateur.

"No."

Was she a jealous god? Or— "Ssoroghod, were you exiled?"

"No and yes. There was a professional quarrel, my view against the galaxy's. I could not return until I knew answers I could show. So, here I am returned, and the answer is that I was wrong. What else must you know, intrusive creature?"

As an invitation to go away, that was hardly subtle. I asked instead, "Why did you Chirpsithra contact Earth?"

"I knew nothing of it. It was not my decision," Ssoroghod said.

"We went to the Moon, and came back, and stopped. We were fiddling with DNA, but we weren't doing it in any lunar dome. I was just old enough to see how stupid that was, and I couldn't do anything about it," I said. "You saved us. Why?"

"Merchants," said Ssoroghod. "They follow their own rules. You might have something of interest to entities with other forms of wealth to trade. So they interfere."

"I owe them," I said. I drank an unspoken toast to the Whee-Nisht.

"Dispenser, it may be you would have come to your senses. Experiments done in your own living space are lethal. You might have explored your Moon under pressure of fear, built your domed city and your nearby protected laboratories, and saved yourselves. You can never know."

I knew.

Ssoroghod said, "And the Whee-Nisht might have accepted my island despite the cost. I could not rob them of the chance! They chose convenience over adventure, short term over long. I gave them most of my lifespan, and they threw it away. I will beg a ride home and make another life for myself." She strode over to a tableful of Chirpsithra crew and began to talk.

And I made myself another Irish coffee, but it was my own species I toasted.

THE MISSING MASS

Midmorning Saturday, the fourth day after the landings, the Draco Tavern was frantic.

You never can tell how the biorhythms of a score of alien species will interact after the landers come down. None of them cycle through exactly twenty-four hours unless they medicate themselves. The first two days I'd been swamped in the mornings. The evenings had been half dead.

Gail, Jehaneh, and Herman were all on duty. Nearing noon, they seemed to have it under control. I could almost relax.

The Draco Tavern is all one room. During the remodeling the bar became a ring in the middle set higher than the main floor, to give me a chance to look around. This many disparate life-forms don't always get along. I've learned diplomacy. I've got stun gear too.

Four Low Jumbos huddled close around a table, almost hiding it. Low Jumbos like crowds. They only show up when there's no room for them. Their bodies shook; the roar of their laughter leaked through the privacy shields as a synchronized bass *huf huf huf*. Their combined bulk nearly hid an entity their own size, the

Terminator Beaver working with his computer against the west wall.

Ten Bebebebeque, sixteen-inch-tall golden bugs, perched around the rim of a table conversing with a Chirpsithra and a gray-and-pink jellyfish in a big glass tank of foamy water . . . big enough to crush my table, it looked like, so it must be sitting on a magnetic float. The jellyfish was new to me. Harsh blue light shone down from the top of the tank, illuminating an intricate internal structure and five dark, wiry tentacles knotted at the center. Evolution beneath a hot, fast-burning sun would explain why they hadn't adapted to the land . . . if there was land where they evolved. Water worlds seem to be common.

Jehaneh set a tray on their table. The water creature used skeletal waldo arms to move a pink canapé through its little air-lock. I watched the canapé slide into its translucent interior.

Jehaneh came back to the bar, looking pleasantly bemused. "Carpaccio flavored with sea salt," she said. "Do all the seagoing forms want red meat?"

"Mammal meat is higher energy than they're used to. They all have to try it, but it makes them hyper. Sometimes they get sick."

"I need four more sparkers," she said, "and four bull shots."

There were Chirpsithra at most of the tables. They're the ones who use the sparkers, and they make and run the interstellar ships. They look like attenuated crustaceans, three meters tall and higher, and are red like a boiled lobster.

Four humans in Arab robes settled around a table. Iraqi seem to have rediscovered the pursuit of wisdom. Aliens made overtures, and they broke into pairs. Two joined the Low Jumbos. Two took high chairs to talk to a Chirpsithra.

A man stopped in shock in the double door airlock.

He didn't look like the usual run of xenobiologist or diplo-mat. Short, pale of skin, oriental eyes, straight black hair going gray, a comfortable old suit and weird tie, a laptop computer hanging from one hand. He wore the vague look of a scholar with a wandering mind. It took him a moment to recover his aplomb.

Then he made his circuitous way toward the bar, shying wide of aliens, *way* wide of the Folk, who laughed at him with lolling tongues, like a pack of wolves with their heads on upside down.

I was human. He was really, really glad to see me. He set the computer on the bar and asked, "Can you make me an Irish coffee?" English accent overlaid on something oriental. Having second thoughts, "Leave out the whiskey."

I told him, "I can do coffee any way you want it, or espresso, cappuccino—"

"Cappuccino would be perfect."

He didn't try to talk over the shriek of live steam. He opened his laptop and booted it up. In the sudden quiet that followed he said, "I'm Roger Teng-Hui. I'm looking for someone."

I asked, "Human or alien?"

"E-mail correspondent," he said. "I'm looking for Helmuthdip." He turned the Toshiba around. He had World Online up and running.

I read an e-mail message from **<Helmuthdip@starlink.net>**:

If the Chirpsithra have such a power source, they may be willing to share it. A Human diplomat might ask.

I asked him, "Power source?"

"He thinks the Chirpsithra are using the energy of the vacuum."

I let that crypticism go past me. "When did you first contact this 'Helmuthdip'?"

"Wednesday evening."

"What's he want?"

"He seems to want me to put political pressure on the crew

from that starship! At first he didn't mention politics, interstellar or otherwise. I took him for human."

The Chirp liner *Scrilbree Zesh* had been in place near the Moon last Tuesday morning. The landers were down before Wednesday noon. Give "Helmuthdip" a couple of hours to buy a computer in Forelgrad and play with it a little. . . . I said, "The timing's tight. You don't know the species?"

"I thought he was human! He had a Web site up, a discussion group on the problem of the missing mass. My filter program caught it. The site didn't look active. It was just him."

I waited.

"I didn't think I was dealing with a political pressure group. He *knew* things. He was *interested*. You know, a dedicated astrophysics site would have been *easy* before the Chirpsithra came. I've been teaching on PBS and the Net for twenty years. Most of my students have disappeared, and I'm the only teacher left."

Herman asked for Arabian coffee for the Iraqis. He took the tiny cups and went off, and I said, "I suppose the problem is that the Chirpsithra know it all."

Teng grimaced. "Do they really?"

"They say so. Their passengers say so. Sometimes they play jokes. I might buy that they know everything they want to," I said, "and what they don't know, their passengers know, and when they don't, they bluff. I'm used to it. I never thought about it from a teacher's viewpoint, but . . . it must be like everybody's sitting around waiting for the answers!"

"Flipping to the back of the book. Give me another cappuccino. Grand Marnier on the side. Do they ever make mistakes, or are all of these entities too advanced?"

"Oh, they make mistakes." A qarashteel had come to Earth to make cheap war movies . . . but I shouldn't blurt *that* out to just anyone. "Your alien would still have had to learn how to use the Internet. Maybe a human being showed him. Let me try something,"

I said. I linked into the Britannica's universal encyclopedia site, found what I wanted, and turned the screen around.

" 'Helmuth speaks for Boskone.' Early science fiction. Helmuth was a space pirate, and a 'dip' is a pickpocket. You're looking for a spacegoing petty thief. Excuse me." Things had gotten busy around the big table, and I went off to deal with it.

The Draco Tavern has always been as much a fast-food joint as a bar, but our supplies and capabilities have expanded over the years. We charge too much because we have to keep too much stuff around, and we have to be too careful what happens to it. Most of this stuff would poison most of the life-forms we get in here, and that *does* include the booze.

A Chirpsithra knew me, though I didn't recognize her. You can't tell Chirps apart; they're gene-engineered to identical perfection. I gestured at the Low Jumbos and asked her, "Do they like crowds that much? Or should I be getting bigger tables?"

"You would not see the end of that endeavor! These"—something breathy—"are not the largest of our clients!"

Other Chirps chittered laughter. One said, "There are life-forms that would not fit in any imaginable vehicle!"

The other, "But were they sapient? How could we ever know?"

Chirpsithra obscurities. I moved on. We were frantic for the next hour.

Then the Iraqis all rose and went out—prayer time, I guess—and suddenly most of the bar was getting up and walking, rolling, lurching, slithering through the airlock into a horizontal glare of Siberian tundra. The Low Jumbos followed the rest.

The jellyfish in his aquarium was still there. I wondered if he'd been abandoned. Five Chirpsithra who had watched their alien companions all go away now gathered around the big table with the aquarium in the center. Herman glanced my way for permission. I thumbs-upped him. He pulled up a high chair and joined them. Something hairy came out of the restroom, looked around at the empty bar, then joined Herman and the chirps and jellyfish.

Jehaneh looked tired. I told her to go sack out. Gail went too. Roger Teng-Hui was still at the bar working his Toshiba. The Terminator Beaver was deeply involved with his Macintosh.

I stopped at the Beaver's table.

What showed of him was largely prosthetic. Under all the goo and wire and silver plating and small glowing icons the Terminator Beaver might have been a solitary Low Jumbo. He was half covered in tiny black platelets, half pink hide bared for prosthetics. Circuitry, lenses, armor covered his body. The material shone like glass and metal and jelly, but it all flexed. There was a narrow indicator strip above his small, neat carnivore's mouth, where he could read it with goggles like two silver eggs. The widgetry had a functional beauty implying, I thought, centuries of design. It hid most of his face.

Wires ran from a neck ring into the ports of the Macintosh. The screen was dancing, flickering, and his fingers never went near it.

He'd told us his name: a near-supersonic birdsong. He had been in the Draco Tavern since the landings, eating and drinking alone. He had bought the Macintosh laptop computer in Forelgrad, the merchant town that has grown up around the spaceport. Gail had shown him the basics during a dull evening. He'd become skilled very rapidly.

We'd speculated. The Draco Tavern's elaborate restroom isn't gender-specific, so we still didn't know *that*. Was he, she, it a cyborg by choice, a medical patient, geriatric case, augmented athlete? Was he an injured Low Jumbo avoiding eyes that might find him ugly?

He'd plugged his Mac into the wall, not into one of the universal sockets the Chirpsithra gave us, but into a telephone jack. I looked back toward the bar. Teng-Hui was around the other side, not visible.

The Beaver might well be the mysterious **<Helmuthdip@starlink .net>**. Did I want Teng-Hui to know that? Did I want to tell the Beaver about Teng-Hui?

I try not to get myself or the Tavern involved in these dominance games. Sometimes there's no helping it. And sometimes I can supplement our income by learning something valuable. I once went broke building a supercomputer, but that's also how I patented the magnetic float.

The game the Beaver was playing wasn't an action game, so I felt free to interrupt. "Terminator Beaver," I said, and let my translator whistle his name, "how are you doing?"

Let him take it either way: progress on the game, or was he thirsty?

He whistle-sang. His translator said, "Dead. Notice joke. I begin the game dead."

"Your character can still get hurt." He was playing *Grim Fandango* upgraded for 3-D. I watched him trying to deal with the coroner and his flower beds. "Do you enjoy hints?"

"No."

"I need a hint to a puzzle. How good are you with that thing?"

"A fascinating toy."

"Have you had dealings with this entity?" I showed him the net address: **<Helmuthdip@starlink.net>**.

He asked, "Do you have access to this entity?" He typed it on the screen: **<chinaRoger@wol.com>**.

"It may be. Describe what you want of him."

"A matter of negotiations. Rick Schumann, why should I tell you more?"

" 'ChinaRoger' hasn't dealt with aliens."

"You have had much experience. I have funds if you will act as a mediator," said the Terminator Beaver.

"I've done that," I acknowledged. "How difficult is my task to be? Try to describe what you want of 'chinaRoger.' "

"I seek knowledge that would point to energy for industrial purposes."

Guessing, I asked, "Something to do with the missing mass?"

"I wondered if you merely pretended to knowledge. Would you accept one-over-twelve-cubed of net profits from this process over the next thousand years?"

I negotiated for half that, plus a modest thousand credits to be transferred at once. A bird in the hand, etc. The recording would serve as a contract if I brought these two together. I hadn't decided on that. Either way, I expected no profit from this.

Herman was getting recharged sparkers for his table. The Wheesthroo, the hairy guy, wanted an orange sherbet shake in odd proportions. I made that and Herman took it away.

Teng had waited patiently. I asked him, "What do you want with this 'Helmuthdip'?"

"I want to know what *he* wants with *me*."

"What's he say he wants?"

"That's complicated."

"I'm not busy."

"I thought he was just another astrophysicist. But, look, I'm *Roger Teng-Hui*. Any decent astrophysicist knows who I am, and I'd know who he was. I don't mind 'Helmuthdip' hiding his name. But he knows of research I've never heard of, and there are terms he didn't know. *That* was funny. He wanted to talk about the expanding universe, but he didn't know 'Hubble constant.' He knew 'missing mass,' but he didn't know 'Casimir effect.' "

"I don't either."

"Ah. Look, this is fascinating stuff—" He caught himself. "Even now. Rick, the current most interesting question in astrophysics is, what is the nature of the expansion of the universe? Will the universe expand to infinity, or will it collapse back to a point? Most astrophysicists would like to find just enough matter to make space flat.

"Understand this picture? If the universe is too massive, it'll expand for a while and then fall back into a reverse Big Bang. If there's not enough mass, it'll be expanding toward infinite volume. Right between, it expands to a finite limit. That's flat space, right between infinite expansion and an eventual collapse, and it fits a cluster of theories built around an inflationary universe. How fast we're expanding is the Hubble constant."

I did in fact understand him, but he didn't wait to find that out, he just raced on. "Now, the right amount of matter to do that depends on how fast the galaxies are going away from each other . . . the Hubble constant, right? The faster they're flying apart, the more energetic the Big Bang explosion must have been, and the more mass it will take to pull everything to a stop.

"The point is, none of the astronomers can find enough mass to do the job. Maybe we would have. Telescopes were getting better all the time, but then the Chirpsithra showed up—"

"Is this what was going on at 'Helmuthdip's' Web site?"

"Yes. I thought he was an amateur at first. Brilliant amateur. I was intrigued.

"The latest, most accurate measurement of the Hubble constant depends on Type 1A supernova explosions. Do you know how *that* works?" I shook my head. "Say you've got a bloated gas giant star losing mass to a white dwarf companion. The hot hydrogen gas rains down through an amazing gravity field, so it's heated to tens of millions of degrees. When it gets dense enough, you get a fusion bomb, *boom.*

"These Type 1A's all resemble each other, and they can be recognized across huge distances. The universe is full of them. A Type 1A supernova tells you how far away it is by how bright it is, and how fast it's moving by its red shift.

"Using those as meters to measure the universe, we get a rate of expansion that suggests around thirty percent of the mass that's needed to close the universe, or ten percent, or seventy percent, depending on who needs a grant."

"So you look for more mass."

"Right! We look in places obscure and weird. We postulate mass we can't see, dark matter, in all sizes from neutrinos to intergalactic dust, to near infinities of brown dwarf stars, to hypothetical massive particles left over from the Big Bang itself. I wasn't a front-runner in all this, but I kept track. And I got old, and we had too many solutions and none of them made a lot of sense. Aliens came down in Siberia, hordes of them, and *they know.* So what was the point?

"Then 'Helmuthdip' popped up on my screen. And for a while he was making sense, and then he got into the Casimir effect."

"What brought you here?"

"And then he started insisting that I use my *influence* on the pilots of an interstellar liner! *That* would have brought me here anyway, but *what* influence? If he comes from a place where astrophysicists have more power than fucking politicians, it's for damn sure he's from interstellar space! But I have to tell you about the Casimir effect."

"Do you really?"

"Actually," he said, "no. Let's leave it that there's energy in the vacuum. Fantastic levels. Space isn't really empty, it's a froth of virtual particles appearing and annihilating each other faster than any hypothetical instrument can detect them, and that's where the energy is. It's been demonstrated mathematically that if the vacuum in free space was empty of energy, you'd have *minus* energy near a black hole.

"The Casimir effect is an experiment that *measures* vacuum energy. You machine two plates very flat, and you move them very close together. They pull at each other—"

"Gravity?"

"No."

"Oh."

"It's done with virtual particles. Virtual particles flash into existence and annihilate each other everywhere in space. But you put these plates so close together that the wavelength between the two plates is too small. There's no room for virtual particles to pop up between them. The pressure on the outsides pushes the plates together, and that's the Casimir effect."

"Strong?"

"Tiny. 'Helmuthdip' has been trying to tell me— Is that entity waving at you? The half-mechanical, ah, person?"

The Terminator Beaver was on his feet and coming around the bar. I said, "Terminator Beaver, meet Roger Teng-Hui, also known as 'chinaRoger.' Teng, meet 'Helmuthdip,' aka Terminator Beaver. I believe you have much to discuss."

They sat at the bar with their computers in front of them, sometimes activating displays to supplement the Chirpsithra translators. They both kept slipping into jargon, then remembered that they were talking to the bartender too. Sometimes it takes a third party to get two people talking the same language.

"The Chirpsithra won't discuss what powers their star-to-star liners," the Terminator Beaver said. "Our landers are various and we build them ourselves, but the liners have apparent infinite power and not enough fuel storage."

"Antimatter?" Teng asked.

"Antimatter they keep for attitude jets, with dross from re-fined sewage as reaction mass. Our *landers* use antimatter. Spies have identified a system aboard *Scrilbree Zesh* for *making* antimatter! Where do they get the energy? Many species wish to solve the puzzle. Sometimes we cooperate. We know that the liner's mass varies during a voyage, losing and gaining again."

"The energy of the vacuum is thinly spread," Teng said.

"By some measurements," the Beaver agreed. "Some theories render it huge. The Casimir effect may measure only the least of what is available."

I saw fit to cut in. "Near-infinite energy in the vacuum," I said, "and near-infinite energy in these huge Chirpsithra ships. That isn't all of your argument, is it? Because they don't have to be related."

They both tried to interrupt. The Beaver's translator cried, "No, no, no! What of the missing mass?"

"He was doing that before," Teng said. "It's an interesting . . . notion."

"We must suppose that early Chirpsithra—" The Beaver saw us about to object. "No? Then think of engineers who find a way to attain the energy of the vacuum. When work is done, some-thing always disappears, does it not? Not energy nor potential nor mass, unless one into the other, but something is gone."

"Entropy," Teng said. "Disorder increases. Energy becomes less available."

"Yes, but what is gone when energy is taken from the vac-uum?" The Beaver's silver goggles flickered as he studied our faces. "You cannot pull energy from the same volume over and over!" he snapped. "Vacuum must disappear!"

I said, "Okay—"

"They learn the ultimate secret, these Engineers. They may be the first of many. Their numbers and ambitions expand. Peculiar and active galaxies may show their work. There is no missing mass," the Beaver said. "The universe is expanding too fast, the Bang was too energetic, but expansion slows because space is disappearing. In the limit, space will be flat."

I asked, "Teng? Is this even sane?"

The man said, "Oh . . . sane. Look, there's no way you can take the same energy out of the same block of emptiness forever. Energy has to become less available. *Sure* something has to go, and it's probably volume. Space shrinks where the Engineers have passed. Why the Chirpsithra?"

"Look about you. *They* have such a power source! How many suspects can you identify?" the Beaver demanded, rather unfairly, since the bar had been nearly emptied.

Teng said, "Well, that's my point. This universe has had around ten to the tenth years to produce a species capable of using the energy of the vacuum. We expect the universe to last . . . how long before interesting things stop happening? Ten to the fortieth years? Ten to the ten to the eighty? We are in the earliest moment of the universe. Most of time is in front of us. The Engineers might not even have a planet to evolve on yet! They may evolve after all the protons have disappeared."

I said to the Beaver, "You have asked the Chirpsithra, haven't you?"

"To us the Chirpsithra said nothing. To another race they once said that the secret of their drive was to be taken as a puzzle. 'Just another cursed intelligence test.'"

Teng burst out, "Your damn hypothesis isn't even falsifiable!"

I asked, "What?"

"When you've got a decent theory, you try to falsify it, Rick. You don't want someone else making you look like a fool, so you try to disprove it yourself first. If a statement *can't* be disproved, falsified *if* it's false, it's useless. Beaver, if the Engineers won't start chewing up galaxies for a trillion trillion years, what evidence would you expect to find *now*?"

"Any species may ask."

"Not us," Teng said, suddenly bitter. "There weren't even human footprints on Mars when the Chirpsithra came. If ever there are, they'll be around a Chirpsithra landing site. Passengers. Why would they give *us* an interstellar drive? We can't even build landers, and they use antimatter just for reaction jets!"

I made two cappuccinos while I thought. All talk stopped in the scream of steam.

It seems I'm doomed to spend my life with entities brighter and more knowledgeable than myself. They gather to talk, all these different shapes and minds, and I am privileged to listen. I love it. But sometimes they talk and talk, and never act.

A mathematician once told me that all of math is a mind game. The strangest thing is that any of mathematics can be fitted into the way any part of the universe behaves. The huge vacuum energies that fall out of mathematical formulations needn't be taken seriously. I knew that without ever seeing the equations, let alone being able to read them.

Then again . . . "Come with me," I said. "Let me do the talking. Teng, you may not know it, but any ongoing conversation should not be interrupted. It's a custom."

"Right. What have you got in mind?" But I was in motion, and what I had in mind was very little.

The big table was down to Herman, three Chirpsithras, the silent Wheesthroo, and the big jellyfish in his aquarium jar. I placed the cappuccinos and pulled up high chairs for the rest of us. One of the Chirps was chittering. My translator said, "Not all of the life-forms known to us enter the Draco Tavern. Poseidon masses as much as *Scrilbree Zesh* itself." *Scrilbree Zesh* was the big ship still orbiting the Moon.

The jellyfish spoke like a snore. Its translator asked, "But this entity could visit Poseidon?"

"One of our ships might cross to Poseidon's world. We would prefer to visit Poseidon before he dies. Wait but a moment." The Chirp's monitor strip twinkled.

Herman took the opportunity to half-whisper, "We've been talking about water worlds. That's Scylla. Nothing to trade, but supposed to be a poet. Poseidon lives on a water world not far from here. He's *huge.*"

The Chirp said, "No such voyage is now planned. Learning to talk again to another of his species would be tedious, but we estimate Poseidon's life span in the thousands of years."

"But mine is not," Scylla the jellyfish said.

"We are sorry. Greeting, Rick."

"Greeting, elder. Greet Roger Teng-Hui and the Terminator Beaver."

"Greet you both. Greet Scylla, whose kind only recently made fire. A great accomplishment it was."

We spoke; the translators spoke; talk grew raucous, then stalled. Into a moment's pause I asked, "What's the largest life-form the Chirpsithra know of?"

"Extinct now," the Chirp said. "They were larger than galaxies. They formed the galaxies. Your telescopes will one day be powerful enough to watch them. Would you witness this now?"

Teng wanted to speak. The Beaver wanted to speak. But they both looked at me first, and Scylla's snore rang out. "Please show us this wonder."

"Our monitors . . . but you have a local computer, I see." The creature's long red armored hand reached out for the Beaver's

Macintosh computer and opened it facing the jellyfish. "Do not disconnect." The Chirp produced a little box of its own and plugged it into a piece of the Beaver's equipment. Her fingers played over a surface.

The Beaver was still attached; he twitched. The Mac's screen raced, went black, then blue-white. "Fast-forward," the Chirp said.

We watched. A wash of violet light dimmed to blue, to green, to yellow, then broke into an expanding chaos of filaments and dimmed further.

The Chirp's translator spoke. "Roger Teng-Hui, how do galaxies form?"

Teng said, "It's a puzzle. Current attempts to model the early universe usually give us a universe that is too uniform to form galaxies. Inflationary theories make galaxies more likely. It's one of the attractive things about inflation."

She said, "You have not yet seen the universe forming. It *was* too uniform. Without galaxies there would be few stars, yet galaxies would never form. But like all here—even Scylla, whose sealocked kind breed transparent jellyfish to make ever more powerful telescopes—we became able to watch."

Out of the chaos came whirlpools of light.

"It may be you cannot see the mechanism. Teng, your people have wondered about the missing mass." Teng recoiled; she chittered laughter. "What is unfalsifiable might still be proven true."

"You've been eavesdropping," I said.

"Our translators note key phrases, as 'missing mass' in conjunction with 'energy of empty space.' If engineers must use the power in the vacuum, and those engineers are yet to evolve, then they will be undiscoverable. But these life-forms we call the First-born evolved very early. They *metabolized* the energy of the vacuum. Wherever there was a bloom of Firstborn, an orgy of uncontrolled breeding, there too were sudden concentrations of mass. Disappearance of volume leaves mass behind, yes? There sudden stars flowered.

"We would study the Firstborn further, but we cannot find them. We fear them extinct. During formation of a galaxy the rage of light and heat may kill them, or else matter around them might grow denser until a black hole swallows all and remains behind to anchor newly forming stars.

"Yet we hope that they still survive between galactic clusters. See this great emptiness—" She showed us on the Mac, a vast hole in the universe where there were no galactic clusters. "We have never traveled that far. If we could study the Firstborn, we might learn their secret."

The Beaver demanded, "But what drives your ships?"

"Our ships use a lesser effect. The Firstborn hold the key to vast wealth. If we have not learned it, *we*, in our billions of years . . . well. Some younger race might. Teng, Beaver, Rick, it is not in our interest that you should give up striving."

Scylla's magnetic floatplate floated out from under the table, and she drifted out onto the tundra. The rest followed. I watched them go, thinking that we must be a common thing to the Chirpsithra. A civilization is only beginning to learn the structure of the universe, when interstellar liners appear and alien intelligences blurt out all the undiscovered secrets.

Primitive peoples die when powerful intruders mock their lifestyles. Whole worlds might be saved, if Chirp diplomats can be trained to imply that vast secrets remain untapped, awaiting the touch of young and ambitious minds.

"Paid you too much," the Beaver told me. "Did you *see* animals the size of a galaxy? I did not. I saw blobs and colors." He ambled out.

Teng caught up with him. I heard him say, "Let's think about expanding that 'Helmuthdip' Web site. Get some of my colleagues involved. Maybe some passengers too." Teng was bouncing, his spirits restored. In a young universe there were still wonders to achieve, secrets for a young species to learn.

THE CONVERGENCE OF
THE OLD MIND

Among the aliens who travel with the Chirpsithra are some who like it cold. Over the years a succession of ice-blooded species have imposed their aesthetic views on the Siberian tundra that surrounds the Draco Tavern. What we can see through the glass wall includes winding paths and a vastness of wonderful statuary carved from ice. Some of the sculpture houses alien storehouses and offices.

Through that barren, desolate, weird landscape I watched two ten-limbed spiders cloaked and hooded against the cold, picking their way through the winding paths.

Those would be Gray Mourners: Sfillirrath and one of her husbands. Sfillirrath, the larger, seemed in haste: she was taking short cuts through the sculpture, leaving her mate behind. She stopped by the biggest airlock and slowly folded herself and all those long legs into it.

The airlock revolved and she was in. Here and there, sensory clusters turned. Sfillirrath spoke a complicated phrase.

She hadn't spoken loudly, but she can't. My translator decided she'd shouted: "The Old Mind is gathering!"

Most of the tables in the Draco Tavern had privacy bubbles enabled. Most of the patrons heard nothing. But nine Bebebe-beque, lined along the rim of the bar in front of me, tumbled off and streamed toward her.

Chittering questions, the six-inch-tall golden bugs followed her to a table full of Chirpsithra. She spoke, they spoke, all in the silence of a privacy bubble. Four tall and spindly chirps got up, leaving one behind, and made for an airlock. The bugs stayed.

The Gray Mourner male reached the big airlock and folded himself through it.

Sfillirrath and her husbands had been hanging around Earth for two years now. *Chimes In Harmony* was newly arrived, currently hovering near the Moon. Sfillirrath had been aboard last night. What she carried would be the latest news, whatever it meant.

It seemed to mean a lot. Patrons watched her approach, listened, then . . . something changed. A few left. But—it took me a while to get it—nobody was talking to each other any more. In Sfillirrath's wake, they were talking to tiny or embedded communication devices.

I stayed at the bar as Sfillirrath circulated among the tables. This might not be any of my business. Then again, would I ever have come here if I weren't curious? I considered speaking to the sole remaining Chirp. As part of *Chimes'* crew she'd know—

But she too was talking to an entity not present.

Sfillirrath was talking to two Folk—and Gail was on her way to offer food or drink or service. Good girl. I'd ask Gail what she'd heard, later. Meanwhile Sfillirrath's mate had reached the bar.

He surrounded a stool, settled some of his mass on it, and spoke. My translator knew the Gray Mourner speech well. It said, "Hot liquid with much sugar and not much alcohol."

"Fruit flavor?"

"No."

I poured him hot tea with Benedictine in it. I asked, "Which are you?"

"You cannot perceive? I am Shkatht."

I said, "The Old Mind is gathering?"

"Yes, in the Orion Cluster."

"Who is the Old Mind and what does it gather?"

He stared, I think. Shkatht has too many eyes to tell. "Information," he said, "and intellect. Have you never heard reference to the Old Mind?"

"Never," I said.

He asked, "Have you ever wondered if there are entities older than Chirpsithra?"

I knew of very old entities that were supposed to be extinct. Otherwise— I asked, "How old are the chirps?" He *might* know.

"A hundred million years, they tell us, or a half billion, or more, or less. It depends on where you set the breaks in speciation. They hold all the red dwarves in the galaxy now, they say. Their first world joined their first sun before they knew how to prevent that," Shkatht said. "But the universe is older than that."

"I wouldn't think species last half a billion years."

"No, certainly not species—"

"Shkatht, what is your mate doing?"

"Spreading the word, offering opportunity to all. The Old Mind is converging near the Orion Birthground. *Chimes In Harmony* prepares to depart. Perhaps the Mind will talk."

Orion . . . birthground of stars? The Hubble telescope gave us pictures of fresh young stars and planetars in the Trapezium Cluster of Orion Nebula. I said, "You'll be centuries getting there. You make it sound like a grunion run."

"We will need more than centuries. A convergence doesn't happen all at once. Not many will choose to go. Some passengers will await the next ship. Some who planned to stay over will fight for a berth aboard *Chimes In Harmony*. They're all on their communicators negotiating, changing their plans. What is a grunion run?"

I said, "Fish come up onto shore to mate in the sand. We catch the grunion for food, if we can guess the right night."

Shkatht knotted himself in a laugh. "This is not a grunion run. We go in hope of speaking to the—oldest intelligence—no, not that. Most knowledgeable, it may be. Rick, permit me a question. What would you make of yourself if your options were infinite?"

I'd played such mind games in college. I said, "I'd make myself intelligent enough to decide what else I wanted."

More aliens were leaving.

"Rick, there will come a point for my kind, or for yours, or for any tool-using community that lives long enough, when intelligence may be made arbitrarily large. Can you see the danger in that?"

I said, "If you make a computer too powerful, it absorbs all knowledge and then turns itself off." I'd bought that knowledge the hard way, with my own money, when the Draco Tavern was new.

"Absorbs all available knowledge," the spider man corrected me. "If a computer can reach further, build its own instruments, telescopes, probes, it lasts longer."

"The poor fool who manufactured it still goes bankrupt!"

"Cease to think in terms of makers and owners, Rick. Let yourself be the computer, let you own yourself, let you seek greater intelligence. If you are confined to just one world, or just one solar system, there comes a point at which there is nothing left to think about. The information flow has fallen too far. You could never survive ten billion years."

"It's that old?"

"Guesswork."

"Go on."

"Give up speed of thought. Give up locality. Optimum might be a sluggish flow that sometimes clusters into blazes of brilliance."

I waited.

"We only know the Old Mind in its present state. What we find is a scattering of elements," Shkatht said, "everywhere in the starfield, spread across the universe. These elements signal each other when their distance is less than . . . it varies greatly with intent . . . but let us say five light-minutes apart. Think of them as the cells of a brain."

"Tiny?"

"Elements the size of fine dust, a few million atoms each. They are adrift. They can guide their paths via magnetic fields or light pressure, sometimes up to very high speeds. The further they drift, the less is the intelligence of any grouping, do you see that? Their thought is slow, when every synapse spark takes up to five minutes, sometimes much more. But as elements spread away, their information gathering capability grows. A billion elements scattered through a light-year can become a wonderful telescope, or can engulf an object to study it exhaustively. The Old Mind learns, and from time to time, it converges."

What I saw with my mind's eye made a wondrous picture. I was getting excited. "So. A human brain is, what, ten to the twentieth nerve cells? Say you clustered ten to the *fortieth* elements of the Old Mind in that five-light-minute limit—"

"Too many. It would collapse into a proto-comet. We expect to see ten to the twenty-fifth or so before it all drifts apart, and the distance will be light-years."

"That's still a lot." A billion years of data cluster into a mind, and it thinks about what it's seen. "It kind of drifts into hyperintelligence, doesn't it?" It's done this before, and the memory is there. A mind forms and climbs toward evanescent godhood.

There would be an updating of the records of the universe, a flurry of problem solving, a flowering of new theory . . . vast slow thought. Spaceships passing through the cloud, or even inhabited worlds, might never be noticed, or might be studied atom by atom. After a time the elements drift apart, seeking new input.

There would be no pretense that the Old Mind was a single intelligence, nothing like the illusion that a single mind occupies a human skull. Just mind forming and dissolving, carrying bits of what it's learned, eventually linking again in a different order, in a universe noticeably changed.

No death. Just the drift.

I asked, "Are you going?"

"Sfillirrath has not decided. I think we will go."

Many of the races I meet never expect to grow old. Others never expect to die. Still, "That's a lot of a lifetime," I said.

"We want new races, new viewpoints, something to show an Old Mind. Else it will not converse and we will not learn."

"Uh-huh."

"We want a human being."

I looked around. Usually there are human customers. All I saw were Gail and Antony, my staff. "Kind of sparse today—"

"I have been asked to ask you, Rick Schumann."

My heart thudded hard. "I have this bar," I said.

"You have trainees. The Draco Tavern would continue," Shkatht said. "Rick, your kind has found only the most temporary of longevity techniques. If you were the only human being aboard *Chimes In Harmony,* ship's laboratories would be brought to bear to keep you alive and in good mental health. The Old Mind converges to observe the birthing of stars and free floating planets and other wonders. We can seduce it with new viewpoints."

"You don't even know it'll *talk?*"

Shkatht shrugged, a disturbing sight. "A convergence must evolve the concepts of communication. Some remember from earlier ages. Some won't bother."

"I'll think about it," I said, and I poured him tea with a different liqueur. Shkatht extruded a snorkel from his tremendous mouth and drank.

He asked, "Are you disturbed by the company?"

"I like aliens. Even so, how many humans have you got room for?"

"How many must you have?"

"I'll think about it." Four, well chosen, might be enough to keep each other sane.

"You have little time to think. *Chimes In Harmony* prepares to depart. Passengers are gathering now. Entropy is having its way with you, Rick. Think how long you might live."

I said, "The Old Mind has immortality. It doesn't die. What it knows doesn't die. And if it ever—" I stopped.

Sfillirrath had emptied a bottle of maple syrup. Gail approached her with another. Sfillirrath spoke to her. She listened. Nodded.

Shkatht asked, "Why did you stop talking?"

"Shkatht, it never clusters *all* of itself, does it?"

"How could that be, since twelve billion years ago? It has spread itself across the universe. But we think the Old Mind almost stopped manufacturing new elements, long ago, and we think we know why. It would have become the dominant natural force in the universe. Nothing interesting could happen after that.

"We wonder if it was too powerful for a time. For billions of years following the Old Mind's expansion, we see no sign of other intelligence—"

"Rick," asked Gail, "may I speak to you?"

They took an established science fiction writer from Sri Lanka.

They took the manager of the San Diego Zoo.

They took Gail.

They wanted humans with a record for getting along with minds unlike their own. I hope three humans are enough to keep each other sane.

I didn't go.

After all, I have this bar. All the traffic between Earth and the universe passes through the Draco Tavern.

There have been other convergences of the Old Mind. Other Chirpsithra liners must have gone to visit them. Sooner or later the stories will come home to the Draco Tavern. All I have to do is wait.

CHRYSALIS

After *Apparent Dischord*'s lander docked, the Flutterbies came to the Draco Tavern every day.

The Chirpsithra called its kind something multisyllabic, with a juicy sound. My translator rendered this as "Flutterby." There were seven. They more nearly resembled caterpillars: segmented worms with a couple of dozen frail legs that bunched up near a complicated face with a triple jaw. They weighed half what I did. In Siberian winter they didn't use pressure suits, nor even clothing for warmth, but backpacks rode behind their heads.

They'd enter through the long-and-low airlock and split up. They were gregarious: they mixed with their fellow travelers and humans too. I spent an hour listening to two of them argue philosophy with a grad student from Washburn U, veering over into quantum physics and astrophysics and evolutionary theory, hitting her in stereo, shooting down every theory she raised.

On the seventh day one Flutterby stayed behind when the rest left. She said, "I hope you will hire me to wait on tables."

The idea tickled me. I'd never had an alien working in the Tavern. Besides, I needed a replacement for Gail, who had gone off aboard *Chimes In Harmony* to find the Old Mind and wouldn't be back until after I was dead.

Of course I could see problems. "Your environmental designation—"

"Tee tee asterisk squiggle ool," she said, "but my supplement box compensates." The caterpillar lifted a feeler to tap the flat bag that rode her back. "I can tolerate a tee tee hatch nex ool environment and Earth's temperature and humidity spectrum. Ultraviolet light would be dangerous; will I need to spend time outside?"

"No. Why do you want to do this?"

"My reasons will not harm you nor your dependents. I will work for food and shelter."

I asked, "Are you underage?"

Our translators may have botched that. She said, "I am older than you are. Child-labor laws cannot apply. Wish you to know if I am an adult? Of course not. I am an incipient female, maturity delayed. Wish you to know if I can bind myself with promises? I can."

Aurora didn't have a name until I gave her one.

Aurora worked for scale: there's a union in Mount Forel Town. Still, scale is cheap. My staff has to face daily crises never described outside of old science fiction magazines. They all have doctorates, and they all work for high salaries.

Food and housing might be a problem. Aurora had said that nourishment was covered. Her backbag included a supplement box that would take care of allergies and dietary deficiencies, and the "ool" designation gave her an herbivorous but flexible diet. As for housing, I had to improvise. The food storage lockers under the Tavern are versatile—have to be—so we reprogrammed one of those.

Some of the human anthropologists who came in were surprised and amused. I don't believe any of my alien customers were startled to find Aurora serving their drinks and such, barring one, and that was her own species.

They wriggled in through the long-and-low airlock, all six of them, two days after Aurora started work. They ordered as usual: a green glop, rich in fiber, stored cool but not frozen, and they needed *lots.* I sent Aurora with it. Their eyestalks avoided her, scanned in wide arcs around her and the big bowl of glop, as they slithered toward the long-and-low airlock. One stopped to register a credit to pay for the abandoned order. They didn't speak to Aurora.

Aurora seemed pleased afterward. When I asked her about it, she claimed it was personal, swore it wouldn't affect the Draco Tavern's business, and refused to speak further on the subject.

The Chirpsithra run the interstellar liners. They're talkative creatures who claim to own the galaxy. They do, if you only count red dwarf stars. The Draco Tavern was built according to their plans, partly financed by them too. They're generally eager to help when problems arise. But when something annoys them, I've known them to play practical jokes.

So I try not to bother the Chirpsithra every time I need data. I have other options.

For instance: the translator devices. They have access to a vast library. It's hard to believe that something that fits in a large pocket or small purse carries that much storage, but it certainly doesn't use the computers on the Chirpsithra liners. The liners orbit the Moon. There would be a lightspeed delay, and there isn't.

I think the pocket translators must be artificial intelligences in their own right.

I tried: {Flutterby [with a "species" suffix] + immature + employment} and got this:

Plant-eater, carbon base, rocky/oxygen/water world, G4 sun. Interplanetary-level industry. Immature Flutterbies above sixty-one point eight kilograms may enter binding contracts to perform service. Servants and machinery take one pronoun; citizens take another.

(Slaves were equivalent to machinery? That sounded like a rigid caste system at work.)

{Flutterby + travel} got me too much material, a long lifetime's study. {Flutterby + interstellar travel + contractual} told me what hundreds of the Flutterby species had done to themselves in order to ride the Chirpsithra liners. Armed with that I confronted Aurora.

It was a dead morning: just us two and a sessile creature drinking alone. I asked, "How old are you, Aurora?"

"In Earth orbits, near seventy," she said, "ship time. Longer than that given relativistic effects." She reared up to polish the big mirror over the bar, avoiding my eyes, catching them anyway in the reflection. "We postpone our maturity by chemical means."

"I can see wanting to live a long time," I said. "Why not grow up first?"

"Rick, how can you bear to ask such personal questions of a waitron?"

"Why not?"

"But we are not of similar caste and rank!"

"I'm your boss," I said. "I'd be handicapped if I didn't know something about you."

Her eyestalks telescoped forward and back, studying me. "Very well. Our mature form is little more than a sex organ with wings. We have no digestive organs and little brains. We live ten or eleven days after we emerge from chrysalis form," Aurora said. "I surmise that biotamperers among the Gligstith(click)optok or Chirpsithra might contrive to make an adult Flutterby immortal, and even find some way to keep her from starving. But she would be decoration, not companion. Companions, citizens, *minds* are found only in children. When an elder becomes a chrysalis, she has younger sibs and children of sibs to protect her until she emerges to fly. Over hundreds of thousands of orbits our line has evolved to live longer, to postpone the mating flight so that we may become more capable of defending our genetic line."

"These other Flutterbies, are they your sibs?"

"They are my mating group—wives and husbands," the translator said.

"Why did they leave when they saw you?"

"I have changed caste/rank. They don't know what to do," she said smugly. "They can order service of me, but only in context of our positions. Else they cannot speak to me, cannot persuade me to . . . persuade me of anything."

"What would they want from you?"

"To go home."

"Then what? Set your metabolism running again? Become an adult?" She avoided my eyes. I asked, "Mate?"

"Mate and breed and die," she affirmed.

"What do *you* want, Aurora?"

"Stay here. Work here. Wait until my mating group leaves Earth."

"What if they don't leave?"

"Their berths are aboard *Apparent Dischord*. They would lose those, as will I. When the next ship arrives, I may try to get a berth. Then again, your Draco Tavern is a convergence of voyagers. Here I would find a life as interesting as theirs."

The Flutterbies boycotted the Draco Tavern for about four months.

Then, on a day when rumor suggested that *Apparent Dischord*'s time was running short, all six Flutterbies filed in and split into pairs.

The Tavern was crowded. They found conversations rapidly. Corliss and Jehaneh went to take orders and didn't come back.

The philosophy grad student, Berda Wilsonn, had returned with a classmate. They'd chosen a big table, inviting company. A Chirp officer joined them, then two Flutterbies. The others all raised their lift chairs two feet off the floor, to match the height of the Chirpsithra.

I eavesdropped a little. At the Wilsonn table it sounded like they were discussing fear. At other tables Corliss and Jehaneh were both bogged down in conversations, overcomplex orders, discussions of cuisine. . . .

It looked to me like some kind of setup.

Well, if it turned sticky, there were Chirpsithra present. I could turn to them as authorities. I left Aurora behind the bar and went to Wilsonn's table to take their orders myself.

The Chirpsithra said, "Please, will you have an Irish coffee with us, Rick?"

"It's a busy . . . yes, of course, glad to." I dismissed the notion of begging off. The Chirp bore rank markings: she was an officer. If this was a game, I could assume she was a player. I sat down, glanced at Aurora behind the bar.

The Chirp asked, "What are you afraid of, Rick?"

"What, *now?*"

"I mean in the general sense."

"Lots of things," I said. "Pain. Injury. Taxes. Weird new laws. You?"

"Change, death, ignorance," she said. "You have seen how little we Chirpsithra tolerate change, how assiduously we avoid death. We seek knowledge everywhere."

"But don't all living things avoid change and death? And hey, animals generally evolve better senses as they get more complex."

"These are not universals," said the Chirp. "Berda, would you repeat—"

"I said I sometimes have nightmares about making social mistakes," Berda Wilsonn said. "Wouldn't that be fear of ignorance?"

I asked, "What about pain?"

Aurora arrived.

The Chirp officer already had a sparker. I asked for a cappuccino: I'd better lay off the alcohol. While Aurora took our orders, the Flutterbies and the grads talked. I hate that. *Never let a waiter escape* isn't slavery; it just means don't leave the poor waitron standing there while you talk around her. Anyway, the crosstalk was confusing my translator.

Humans, it seemed, were afraid of nearly everything.

Many species were afraid of death. Others feared loss of mind, loss of intelligence. I've hunted with the Folk; I said they were afraid of nothing. Damn few space travelers feared pain; they'd all found ways to block it. Gray Mourners, the males, were afraid of unprotected sex. Flutterbies?

A Flutterby told Aurora, "Green glop, temperature fifty-one degrees," while the other asked the grads, "How would you live your life if you knew exactly when and how you were to die?"

"I remember an old science fiction story like that," the boy, Willis, said. "Martians could see the future but not the past. Their lives just ran down like a windup toy."

Berda said, "I could plan a lot better. My grandmother used to say, 'If I'd known I was going to live this long, I'd have taken better care of myself.'"

Willis asked, "The menu says you can make guacamole?"

"It's already made," Aurora told him.

"Guacamole and Fritos," he said, and she went away.

"There'd be less to be afraid of," the girl said. "Even when you got old, you wouldn't have to worry about falling off a balcony or dodging a bus. The bus either gets you or it doesn't."

"I suggest a different hypothesis," the first Flutterby said. "Presume you know exactly how and when you will die, if you can survive all natural dangers. Your mind will fade first. You will die in ecstasy, and you will be too stupid to know that it's the end for you."

The second said, "The chrysalis form is a deep torpor. What wakes is near mindless. Digestive organs have faded too. There's no motive except survival and mating, and then even those nerves shut down."

The first: "Also you may pause your fate indefinitely. The danger is that all other ways to suffer or die will have more time to find you."

The boy asked, "You're not being hypothetical now, are you?"

"No. This is our fate, but we must still fear all other mischance. Predators, a fall, a misalignment in *Apparent Dischord*'s antimatter containment could rob us of our destiny. We took this risk gladly in order to see more of the universe."

Aurora returned pushing a floating tray.

Willis dipped up some guacamole. I hid my grin with a cappuccino mug; but I'd looked first to see he hadn't found the wrong bowl of green glop. He said, "We do the same."

The Flutterbies seemed startled. "What? Do you really?"

"I mean we try to live as long as possible. Whatever's currently killing our old people, we go through a lot of effort to cure it. That always means the next thing in line gets us. It was cancer and Alzheimer's when I was growing up, because we'd cured some other diseases. Elders usually die miserably, and it sometimes takes a long time—"

"There isn't any good way to die," the girl snapped. She looked at the Chirpsithra. "Is there?"

The Chirp said, "You already know our answer. Some of us are many millions of Earth-orbits old. All sapient beings evade what evolution shaped us for. All meddle with their destiny, even Flutterbies. A Flutterby who succeeds at longevity will not breed. That seems very strange."

"Death comes to all of your kinds, and always unwelcome," the second Flutterby said. "Our death is welcome if we hang on long enough. We've arrested our development, but we took our risk with senses wide open."

The Flutterbies left during a lull in the ongoing ice storm. Afterward Aurora came to me. "I must resign my post," she said.

"You were listening to them, weren't you?"

"Certainly."

"Does it strike you that they were talking *for* you?"

"Oh, yes," said Aurora. "They could not speak to me, but they could convey arguments in my hearing. Also they brought pheromones from adult Flutterbies. I felt protective and protected, and I heard their arguments. I know what they did to me. I know, but it doesn't matter."

"Pheromones. Doesn't that strike you as unfair?" In fact the whole jape seemed monstrously unfair.

Aurora said, "We must have adults about us, to protect. Proper pheromones are released into our cabins during flight. If I remain on Earth I will not have that. I will only have the knowledge that I die without children. But, Rick, their argument cuts both ways. I go to see if they can follow their own logic."

I paid her salary to date, and she went.

Two days later, the Draco Tavern was empty. Corliss went to visit her family in Canada. Jehaneh stayed, of course. With her two passengers—one a visiting sapient bacterium, the other our un-born child—she's grown a bit heavy for travel. And we waited for *Apparent Dischord* to leave the Moon.

Instead, a floating cart parked itself outside the array of air-locks. A Chirpsithra came in and got me, the same officer who'd sat at the Wilsonn table.

I looked into the cart at six fat fluffy white bags each about my size, lightly dusted with fluffy white snow, and one growth-arrested Flutterby.

The Chirp said, "We must ask for judgment. May these im-migrate?"

"I don't make policy for the UN," I said. "What happened?"

"It may have caught your attention—"

I lost patience. "Half my clientele that day were conspiring to get Aurora back to her berth in *Apparent Dischord*. Why?"

The Chirp officer said, "When clients board as a group, we prefer that they remain a group. We do not like to explain how we lost one here, one there. Others of my passengers found it amus-ing to help rebuild a lapsed . . . family."

"Now you've lost all seven," I said. "Aurora? What happened?"

"You heard their arguments. They were sensible," the re-maining Flutterby said, "and I am persuasive. If we—if my mating group were to wait for our return to homeworld, any kind of acci-dent might take us. If we lose even one of seven, our genetic vari-ety might be too sparse. We owe it to our gene line to have our children immediately."

"We? But not you."

"One must remain to teach the children. I may still mate among the next generation."

"Or the one after that. They bought this?"

"Rick, for most of the species I've met, mating has consequences, but not for us. It was not difficult to persuade my family that it is time to mate. My time will come too."

I sighed. I asked, " 'Immigrate'?"

The Chirp officer said, "We don't have convenient room aboard *Apparent Dischord*. Rick, your planet is wide. A few dozen refugees won't harm you."

"What do they eat?"

"Thank you, Rick, an excellent point. We will learn."

At that point I knew I was stuck. I dropped the word to some news channels before I called any government agencies.

The mating dance swirls above the Draco Tavern, gloriously sharing its colors with the Aurora Borealis. They are all brilliant wings and little torso, more kite than butterfly. They mate while falling. Via movie screens and TV sets it is being seen all over the Earth.

Presently they scatter across the tundra. Chirpsithra researchers have found Siberian plants the immature forms can eat, and scent-marked them so the adults can find them.

I'll have to talk to Aurora about food supplies for future generations. The Siberian tundra isn't exactly lush.

THE DEATH ADDICT

T he Draco Tavern was nearly empty: just me and the bugs and Sarah. Sarah was complaining about the expanding universe.

She's an angular woman with solid and elegant bones, not much flesh to cover them. She'd introduced herself to me: Dr. Sarah Winchell, anthropologist, a woman in her forties (a bit younger than myself) who had lived with apes in the wild and had now come to confront aliens. I'd have expected her to be overspecialized. Her knowledge of cosmology surprised me.

I'd brought her two mai tais, with popcorn for the Bebebebeque. Now she was drinking club soda. Her speech stayed lucid and brisk.

"The universe is expanding," she told the ring of bugs. "Fine, I can live with that, I grew up knowing that. But the expansion is *increasing*. Getting faster. What could be the *purpose* in a universe that is forever blowing apart?"

She sat in an arc of chrome yellow bugs each about fourteen inches tall, perched around the rim of the big table. They buzzed.

Their translator said, "Purpose you expected? Examine your contract!"

She laughed.

The Bebebebeque were a hive mind. They spoke with one voice. "To isolate cultures may be a way to keep novelty in the universe. Too easy communication is making the human race too uniform, is it not?"

Sarah laughed again. "We're not uniform!"

"You seem so to us. For purpose, will you have entertainment? The puzzle of how to build civilization changes with time. Tools are invented, then better tools. If this goes on, all problems may be solved, all tools reach their perfect state. It may be that a universal expansion propelled by dark energy is expected to compensate, make communication more difficult, puzzles more interesting. Here enters Bazin; shall we ask him?"

She turned to see who had come through the line of airlocks.

Bazin was an aerodynamic shape. He might have been mistaken for a thousand-pound turtle, but he moved more briskly, even with sixty pounds of life support and sensor gear mounted on his shell. I'd spoken with him when we arranged for CBS to interview him.

Sarah said, "I've seen Bazin on television. Is he, what, a philosopher? Cosmologist?"

The Bebebebeque were amused. "No!"

"I thought he was something like a stuntman. Rick?" She turned to me. "Do you know—"

I said, "Even before *Fly By Wire* made orbit, my customers all knew he was coming." I poured out a row of tiny golden seeds in front of the Bebebebeque, and gave Sarah her water. "Out there among the stars, he's a star. Bazin is a daredevil, a risk taker. Maybe he does some exploring too, but mostly he's looking for the biggest thrill. He makes, um, entertainments. Wire him up and you can record what he experiences. If he ever gets killed, they'll record that too."

I stepped outside the privacy shield around the big table, so he could hear me, and shouted, "Bazin!"

Bazin swerved toward us. The turtle-analogue's own voice was a series of eructations from under his flexible shell. His translator cried, "Rick! What is the topic?"

I said, "The topic is cosmology."

He joined them at the big table. But more customers had come in, so I missed the rest of that conversation.

Most of Earth has to put up with television sets, but the Chirp-sithra had long since set up a huge holo wall in the Draco Tavern. Generally we let it jump randomly between news channels. Bazin was with us a few days later, while we watched the *Today* interview.

"I haven't decided what I'll do on Earth," Bazin's image told Wade Hannofer, *Today*'s talking head. "I don't know what Earth has to offer yet, and of course local governments have territorial rights. I welcome suggestions."

Hannofer asked, "Have you seen the Grand Canyon?"

Bazin brushed it off. "I have viewed Valles Marinaris on Mars. When I am done with Earth, I will sail it in a balloon."

"Mons Olympus?"

"Too shallow. A climb would be a mere walk. Maybe I'll climb Everest." In close-up I saw the gleam of his shell, polished to a mirror. The Bazin beside me had lost some polish. A webbing of old cracks showed deep in his shell. I remembered an actor, Jackie Chan, who had a scar for every movie he'd made.

The image of Wade Hannofer waved around at the image of the Draco Tavern. "Some of the visitors here know when they'll die. Some are immortal. What are you?"

"I have longevity," Bazin said. "Nanosurgery has turned off the death wish in my genetics. I may be killed, but I will not die naturally."

Afterward Bazin asked me, "Did you enjoy the interview?"

"They cut too much," I said.

"I was only talking. They'll pay more attention when I test the Earth for its potential."

We watched Bazin as he went about the Earth. My customers came less often, though *Fly By Wire* continued to orbit the Moon.

In Disneyland Bazin took the "Star Tours" ride three times straight.

In a movie theater, the only viewer, he watched *Nightmare on Elm Street, The Thing,* and *Die Hard.*

He made news by riding roller coasters: the tallest, the steepest, the fastest. At all three parks they had to alter a car for him.

The commentators were getting disgusted when Bazin moved into Phase Two. He strung a wire across the Grand Canyon and crawled across it—with a groove stapled to his belly plate, and a small pack added to the gear on his back. We learned later that that was a pop-out hang glider.

He went hang gliding, using his own aerodynamic shape and modified Swim-Fins on his flattened hands and feet to steer toward a target, popping his parachute at the last possible moment.

He jumped from the Brooklyn Bridge with a bungee cord, after elaborate testing.

He went white-water rafting on the Colorado River. The humans wore life vests; he wore artificial gills. When the raft tumbled, his shell bumped rocks until he could recover.

I began to see elements of Bazin's style. He did every dangerous thing in the safest possible fashion.

He must have studied Earth's history of flamboyant stunts.
Most of what we had to offer didn't apply to him. On Earth he
needed life support, but where did life support end and protection begin? With his shell and his low center of gravity and an
oxygen source, he could plod up Mount Everest with no danger.
With sufficient padding he could go over Niagara Falls, and so
what? What is skydiving if you have antigravity?

In his absence the Draco Tavern's clientele discussed his adven-
tures. They told of his testing new forms of armor, ballooning
through a superJovian free floater, skating across a lake of molten
sulfur.

On Earth a chartered aircraft set him down at the South Pole,
with equipment piled on a dogsled and more balanced on his
shell. He walked out over several weeks, pulling the sled. The
huskies he treated as pets.

He walked through Death Valley, carrying a small version of
what they sold in the Sahara and Los Angeles, a device that con-
denses water out of the air. I wondered why.

After seven months' absence, Sarah Winchell came back. The
Tavern was empty. She picked the big table. I brought cappuccinos and joined her.

"I've been on a Stephen King binge," she said.

I said, "He was good."

"I've got his whole library on here." She tapped her book-
plate. "When you spend a lot of time traveling, you need a good
library. Otherwise you'll go nuts. But I've been wondering, why
do we want to be scared?"

A trio of brown-furred quadrupeds with manipulators around their mouths joined us but didn't interrupt. I said, "Maybe we just want to forget what we're really scared of."

Sarah asked, "What would that be?"

I said, "Taxes. Terrorists. Slipping on a rainy sidewalk. Cancer. If we do everything right, we grow old. Well and good. Most star-traveling species know roughly what that means for them. For a Flutterby, it's rebirth as a brainless mating machine, ecstacy before death. For humans, it's swollen joints, failing organs, maybe Alzheimer's. You Horka, you have longevity, don't you? What do you see in your future?"

One of the furry quadrupeds answered, "I see what was always my doom. Bones turned brittle, nerves slowed, until a prey takes me as predator. We only postpone. But other species may postpone forever. They can lose all sense of place, of continuity. Like this one," as a Chirpsithra joined us.

"We're all afraid of some things," Sarah said. "A writer like Ray Bradbury can show you what *he's* afraid of. But there must be horrors we don't even dream about."

One Hork said, "Dream?"

I grinned and left her to explain dreaming. And a shape like an overstreamlined turtle slid through the low-and-wide airlock.

"Bazin!"

"Rick! I see you lack for customers. What's the topic?"

"Fear. What can I bring you?"

He wanted an array of consommés. While he joined the big table, I went for soup, a sparker for the Chirp, and dark beer for the Horka.

When I came back Sarah was saying, "H. P. Lovecraft tried to create the fear of something too big, too powerful, too different, too old. So did Lord Dunsany. Stephen Baxter goes way further. He's not trying to scare you, he just reaches further than most minds can stand."

Bazin asked, "Might you yourself grow too old?"

"Well, those old writers were mostly talking about the past. Wizards a thousand years old, or ten thousand—" The Chirp was chittering laughter and Bazin's head had withdrawn into his shell, but she plowed on. "—Races older than humanity. Old enough that they'd know everything; they'd win any fight using techniques forgotten long ago. It's one way to tell a story."

"It's a sometime truth," Bazin said, "although one would need greater age than that! But what if you yourself were the old one? Ultimately there would be nothing of interest."

She thought about that. "There'd be new things to learn."

The Chirpsithra said, "That is not sure at all. It grows more difficult to hold a civilization together as the universe expands. Have you learned yet that the expansion is accelerating? The galaxies fly apart faster and faster."

"Yes," she said.

"The galaxies themselves evaporate, some stars spinning out of the lens, some dropping into the black holes at the center. In ten billion years I see no possible way to connect cultures. The proton is unstable too. In some vast amount of time we'll have nothing but electrons and positrons all light-years apart, and nothing interesting will happen ever again. Is this not something to inspire fear?"

Sarah laughed. "Would you call that 'existential fear'? It takes too long!"

Bazin poked his head out of his shell. "It certainly frightens me," he said.

"Does it?"

"I cannot even think about it. I certainly do not intend to face it. Can you extrapolate me as the last cluster of protons in the universe? I must have some reassurance that I will not live to see all of this slow to a stop."

Is that why . . . ? I didn't ask, because Bazin was pulling into himself. Horn caps on his knees and skull blocked holes, locking his shell against intrusion. This was what he would look like at the end of the universe.

We next saw Bazin riding a kayak over a succession of waterfalls. Afterward he disappeared into a system of caves in the Mindanao Trench. He hasn't been seen since. We get occasional transmissions.

STORM FRONT

The dome that covers the Draco Tavern can be set to show almost anything. It can be a window. It can show recordings across the whole dome, or break up into dozens of frames. We can get live feeds from anywhere in this world or others. Moving among the tables on a busy night, I'm subjected to a bewildering variety of scenery.

Tonight's crew ran to sophisticates: aliens of a wide variety, but they all knew how to use the visuals to tell stories or back up arguments. Worlds danced around me, and obscene medical animations, and fractal geometries. This night had already run more than thirty hours since *Spin Constant*'s lander came down from the Moon. When I got back to the bar, I set the view to transparent just to give my eyes a rest.

The sun was trying to rise, not quite making it in Siberian February; just enough to put a golden glow on the horizon. It washed out other stars, but the new star blazed brightly within the glow.

A Chirpsithra officer folded herself into a chair at the bar. I offered her a sparker. "We came to view that," she said. "It's already in its later stages, but we have good recordings. Ssss," as current flowed through her nervous system. "We saw the neutrino wake and were able to slow down for the best view."

"Is that footage available?"

"Surely, for a price."

We get newsfolk in the Draco Tavern. I'd drop the word.

Beneath the new star, a yellow-white light came rolling across the ice. I waved at it. "Is that one of yours?"

"Not a passenger," the Chirp said. "A refugee."

The visitor rolled in like a big lamp, a five-foot-tall sphere glowing yellow-white, its intensity turned down now. It bumped along the shock-absorbing floor. It was heavy.

That glow must be riding lights, I thought, so that passersby don't get rolled over. If that color had been black-body tempera-ture, the Draco Tavern would have burned. Nonetheless the sphere was hot. As it approached the bar I felt welcome warmth on my face. In Siberia in winter, you never quite get warm enough. Various customers, human and not, turned toward the visitor or expanded their surface areas. Others shied away, of course. The Tavern gets all kinds.

I asked, "What'll it be?" Trusting the translator I was sure it carried.

"Only your company," the visitor said. "You don't store hot plasma, I take it. How strange this place is!"

"Compared to what?"

"Compared to my home. Let me show you." A tendril of light sparked on the thing's surface. In response, a triangular window formed in the dome, shedding blue-white light with whorls in it.

"Damp that," the Chirpsithra officer ordered. The light dimmed. Even so, it would put out too much heat if it stayed on. I tried to guess what I was looking at. "One of those star-hugging gas giant planets?"

"A sun. That sun." A sparkling tendril waved out at the brilliant pinpoint.

The pictures in my head turned over. I was looking at a containment for a plasma confined at X-ray temperatures.

Refugee, the Chirp had said. I said, "Sorry."

"There was a plague," the refugee said. "A self-replicating magnetic effect that damps us from the inside. Before we could control it there were only eleven of us left. Too few, far too few, to regain control of our weather. *Spin Constant* came in the last breath of time to save nine of us."

The Chirp said, "We'll be able to read out their memories with a few years of study. That won't sell to just anyone."

You can hear, and sometimes you can buy, peculiar nightmares in the Draco Tavern.

I flinched from increasing the refugee's pain, but he seemed willing to talk. I asked, "Weather?"

"The weather in a star can become chaotic, out of balance. Like that." Again the refugee gestured at the nova in Earth's sky. The sunset light had died, and it had become more brilliant yet, with shock-wave patterns traced around it.

To the Chirpsithra, I said, "That's too close for comfort, isn't it? Close enough to hurt *us*."

"We can sell you some shielding," she said.

"Good." Of course someone would have to explain this matter of cosmic rays and a ruined ozone shield to professional politicians in the United Nations. It would be like talking to handicapped children, but otherwise the funds wouldn't emerge.

I decided that wasn't my problem. I asked the refugee, "What will you do now?"

"We hope to settle in Sol, if the locals make us welcome."

"Sol?" *Our* sun. "Locals?"

The Chirp was amused. She asked me, "Did you think the

steady weather in your star was an accident? Most stars on the main sequence have a population that knows at least rudiments of weather control. Any telescope can tell you whether they do it well or badly. In Sol they're a little clumsy. Bigger stars are harder to control. In their twilight years an intelligent species can lose the balance. Then there are novas and other disturbances."

I nodded as if I'd known that all along. "Would they, the locals, be interested in talking to us?" It seemed unlikely that they would visit the Draco Tavern, or come to this cold rock at all. But they'd have knowledge to contribute, and who knows? Human mathematicians and computers might contribute something their Weather Department could use.

The Chirp said, "I'll speak to them when we negotiate for Fireball," indicating the refugee, "and his people. That won't be soon. We should quarantine them for a bit to be sure they're not contagious."

An anthropologist was signaling for a refill—gin and tonic, she being human—and I turned away to make it. But the word sat in my head like a time bomb. Contagious. Contagious?

. . . Beings deep within the sun, all dead of Fireball's magnetic contagion. How would we know? We'd never detected them when they were alive. The sun a vast graveyard, sunspots boiling uncontrolled across the photosphere, X-ray-temperature storms forming deep within. Masses sinking toward the center, temperatures rising . . . the sun rings like a great gong . . .

I asked, "How long a quarantine?" and turned around.

But the Chirpsithra officer and his fiery refugee had gone off to another table.

THE SLOW ONES

He landed a small plane at the Mount Forel Spaceport, with a lot more runway than he needed. He'd phoned ahead. I watched him for a while, making his way on foot along the three-kilometer path that leads down to the Draco Tavern. He took his sweet time, stopping to pan across the alien foliage with the video-camera bump on his forehead.

When he stopped to rest, I went out to meet him. What the heck, the Tavern was clean and in good repair and life was turning dull.

This strip of land between the airlocks and the foothills is covered with strange plants, purple ground cover too dry to be moss, and big odd shapes that you might take for wind-shaped rocks. He was looking about him, delighted and a little awed, as he perched on one of the slow ones. This one looks like a rock wind-smoothed into the shape of an inverted boat. I was amused.

"Thank you for letting me come, Mr. Schumann," he said. He was a black-haired white American, medium height, with a smile that might have been ingratiating. The vid camera was a glittering dot on his forehead. "Matthew Taper. I'm with CDC Network. I hope I won't keep you long."

"No problem. There aren't any ships in and I've got lots of free time."

"Ah. Good." He slid over to make room for me on the Type Two Slowlife. I sat. He hadn't noticed a second inverted-boat-shaped rock, this one's mate, fifty meters further back.

He pointed at a cube of clear yellow plastic set in the Draco Tavern's wall. There was a shadow inside it: a dark aerodynamic shape like a large turtle with big clawed feet and a head partly retracted. Taper asked, "Is that an alien or a sculpture? Or a hologram?"

"Alien," I said. "Speedy, I've been calling it. It's almost through the jelly lock."

"That's an airlock? Made of *jelly*?"

"They're all airlocks, that whole line along the front of the Tavern. For Speedy we've got this block of plastic . . . not jelly, just memory plastic soft enough to deform. He'll walk through it, but slowly, and it won't lose air in either direction."

"How many aliens have you got in right now?"

"Ten. Six are in Argentina, hunting."

"But you have to feed the rest?"

"I meant on Earth. There's nobody actually *in* the Tavern."

Taper's eyes defocused: he was consulting notes. "You got a lot more with the first liner, with *Thrill Seeker*. Five species, twenty individuals. That first landing must have been a thrill a minute."

I waved it off. "Oh, you can find anything you want about the first one. Let me tell you about the second landing."

"Weren't there records of that too?"

"But nobody looks at them. . . ."

That long ago, we didn't have much telescope coverage of the Moon. What we had was Spaceguard. Spaceguard was an effort by NASA and other political entities to track Near Earth Objects: that is, asteroid threats above one kilometer across. Map those and you might stand a chance of protecting the planet from a giant meteoroid impact. They'd already found 90 percent of the candidates, they said.

An object was found approaching the Moon's dark limb. It blinked out as it entered the shadow.

Another skywatcher caught the flare of what might have been its drive, but turned out to be riding lights. The skywatching community began talking to each other. Hundreds had it in view when the Chirpsithra liner settled into orbit around the Moon, and they didn't tell a single disaster control office or newsman for nearly ten hours.

They'd done this once before, with an incoming asteroid that turned out to be a false alarm. Skywatchers talked to each other, and the public remained in blissful ignorance. Lines of communication just hadn't been established.

But now the world was watching, and everything happened too slowly. The mile-wide soap bubble drifted in orbit around the Moon. A smaller boat budded loose and drifted toward Earth. Eased down through the atmosphere, taking more hours, following force field lines down to Earth's magnetic pole. It settled at Mount Forel in Siberia, where the first ship's boat had touched down last year.

Everything we saw came via orbital cameras; it was hours before camera crews could get on site. We saw aliens eleven feet tall and very slender, plated with dull red armor: the same Chirpsithra species who had crewed the first ship. They emerged from the lander and began landscaping.

Taper asked, "Was the Draco Tavern in place yet?"

"No, I had backers and a site, but there was nothing on it but posts and string."

"Pity. So what do you mean, landscaping?"

"That's what it looked like, even up close. They sprayed water and dirt and alien fertilizer. I was one of the first on site, and I could smell that chemical reek.

"Cameras showed up, and newspersons, and UN officials. The Chirpsithra went about their business. They planted some weird alien trees in the soil they'd made, and then some structures that they brought out on big float plates. Like Japanese landscaping, we thought."

"I'll run those records after I get home." Taper waved around us. "Is this what you're talking about? This whole three or four square miles looks like alien gardening."

"Yeah. Those bigger trees were planted as saplings. Most of this layered mosslike stuff grew up over the next few years. The slow ones were already in place. There was plenty for the herbivores by the time they got hungry.

"The Chirps talked to me about the interspecies tavern I wanted to build. We settled on where to put it, right at the edge of the cultivated stretch. They left me the jelly lock and a lock for themselves, and those were the first pieces of the Draco Tavern. They played diplomat and gave some interviews, and then they left."

Taper was having trouble catching up. "Slow ones?"

"Originally there were a dozen," I said. "Six little half-eggs must have been food animals. They didn't move fast enough, and the Type One, Speedy, rolled over them and ate them during the first six or seven years. Two of the others went home on the next ship after snuffling around Siberia on tractors. They were the fastest.

"After they left, Speedy was making visible progress toward the airlocks. It's taken him twenty-six years to get into the jelly lock. He'll be inside before Christmas. These others—do you see that tree stump with an indented top? And water in the top, a little pond of his own, but you can't see that. He's the slowest. These boat-shaped—"

"Yeek!" He rolled off.

I stayed where I was. "Ahab doesn't mind. I know them all pretty well. You can talk to them with electronic mail—"

"They can use computers?"

"Sure, all of these slow ones are intelligent tool users. The computers they build work as fast as ours. To the slow ones they're instantaneous. To talk to them you just trade letters. It doesn't matter how slow they write."

I watched him working out how useless that would be to a newsman. I said, "Of course they need terrific protection against spam. Otherwise—"

"Yeah. What do they talk like?"

"Here." I fished out my translator and whispered a few instructions. It projected a screen, watery looking in the horizontal sunlight.

> Hello! I seek a companion.
>
> I am Rick Schumann, human, hoping to become a bartender.
>
> Call me Quizzical.
>
> Hi, Quizzical.
>
> Is that your structure being erected on the tundra?
>
> Yes, that's the Draco Tavern.
>
> Most impressive. I wondered if winds would damage it, but it has stood for some time.
>
> There was some damage two years back. We fixed it.

I hope to see the inside soon. It mutates like dreams.

Be welcome. The jelly lock is for slow ones—

I see it. Speedy is almost there. I see a fluttering that must be your kind's traffic.

Do you know the Chirpsithra?

They live too fast to be truly known, but they don't die too soon. At least we may converse. One, Ktath

Taper scowled. "Is that all?"

"Yeah. Quizzical is the Type Three, the one like a tree stump."

"Twenty-six years?"

"Understand, Mr. Taper, most of my visitors use oxidizing chemistry. Some are even faster than Chirps and Humans. One type burns like a fire. She was born in the Tavern, and I only got to know her for a few hours. But that's not the only way to live.

"Reducing chemistry is very slow compared to oxidizing. These slow ones are exploring the Earth. They watched the Draco Tavern grow up in front of them. They'll see it turn to dust. They'll be here a long time."

Taper rapped what I was sitting on. "This shell—"

"They're in pressure suits. So's Speedy. They have to be protected from oxygen."

"They're all streamlined," he noted. "Even that tree stump has a teardrop silhouette," turning his camera on Quizzical.

I said, "Just being a slow one wouldn't slow down weather. Comes a hurricane, or a flood, they'd just have to wait it out."

Taper asked, "May I talk to Speedy?"

"I'll give you his e-mail address. Have you got a story now? Or is it all too slow?"

"May I have the other e-mail addresses?"

"I'll ask first."

Taper came back in January. This time he hurried through Siberia's endless freezing night to reach the Tavern. The airlock for humans is there because Siberia in winter isn't a habitable planet.

The Tavern was crowded; a liner was in. He stood there taking it in for a few minutes, recording with the camera on his forehead. Then he hung up some of his gear and wove his way through the crowd and the divergent environments.

Speedy was past the jelly lock and ten centimeters inside. Taper smiled down at the smoothed-out turtle shape. He ran a hand over Speedy's head. Then he fished out a keyboard and began typing.

I was at his elbow. "How's it going, Mr. Taper? Got a story yet?"

He laughed. "Not today. If I made a lifetime project of this, I might have something to show the execs. Mr. Schumann, this doesn't take every minute of my time. I've kept four interviews going for seven months without ever skipping lunch. When I'm an old man, these guys could save my reputation."

"This last ship," I said, "brought three more."

"Addresses?"

"They haven't logged in yet. Come back in the summer and I'll introduce you."

Welcome to Earth!

Thank you. We are Bricks, a multiple mind.

Taper, a human.

Can you tell us what of Earth is worth seeing?

Lots! You could watch Niagara Falls eat its way west. Watch redwoods grow. Ride a glacier.

CRUEL AND UNUSUAL

C hirpsithra do not vary among themselves. They stand eleven feet tall and weigh one hundred and twenty pounds. Their skins are salmon pink, with exoskeletal plates over vital areas. They look alike even to me, and I've known more Chirpsithra than most astronauts. I'd have thought that all humans would look alike to them.

But a Chirpsithra astronaut recognized me across two hundred yards of the landing field at Mount Forel Spaceport. She called with the volume on her translator turned high. "Rick Schumann! Why have you closed the Draco Tavern?"

I'd closed the place a month ago, for lack of customers. Police didn't want Chirpsithra wandering their streets, for fear of riots, and my human customers had stopped coming because the Draco was a Chirpsithra place. A month ago I'd thought I would never want to see a Chirpsithra again. Twenty-two years of knowing the fragile-looking aliens hadn't prepared me for three days of watching television.

But the bad taste had died, and my days had turned dull, and my skill at the Lottl speech was growing rusty. I veered toward the alien, and called ahead of me in Lottl: "This is a temporary measure, until the death of Ktashisnif may grow small in many memories."

We met on the wide, flat expanse of the blast pit.

"Come, join me in my ship," said the Chirpsithra. "My meals-maker has a program for whiskey. What is this matter of Ktashisnif? I thought that was over and done with."

She had programmed her ship's kitchen for whiskey. I was bemused. The Chirpsithra claim to have ruled the galaxy for untold generations. If they extended such a courtesy to every thinking organism they knew of, they'd need . . . how many programs? Hundreds of millions?

Of course, it wasn't very good whiskey. And the air in the cabin was cold. And the walls and floor and ceiling were covered with green goo. And . . . what the hell. The alien brought me a dry pillow to ward my ass from the slimy green air plant, and I drank bad whiskey and felt pretty good.

"What is the matter of Ktashisnif?" she asked me. "A decision was rendered. Sentence was executed. What more need to be done?"

"A lot of very vocal people think it was the wrong decision," I told her. "They also think the United Nations shouldn't have turned the kidnappers over to the Chirpsithra."

"How could they not? The crime was committed against a Chirpsithra, Diplomat-by-Choice Ktashisnif. Three humans named Shrenk and one named Jackson did menace Ktashisnif here at Mount Forel Spaceport, did show her missile-firing weapons, and did threaten to punch holes in her if she did not come with them. The humans did take her by airplane to New York City, where they concealed her while demanding money of the Port Authority for her return. None of this was denied by their lawyer nor by the criminals themselves."

"I remember." The week following the kidnapping had been

hairy enough. Nobody knew the Chirpsithra well enough to be quite sure what they might do to Earth in reprisal. "I don't think the first Chirpsithra landing itself made bigger news," I said.

"That seems unreasonable. I think humans may lack a sense of proportion."

"Could be. We wondered if you'd pay off the ransom."

"In honor, we could not. Nor could we have allowed the United Nations to pay that price, if such had been possible, which it was not. Where would the United Nations find a million svith in Chirpsithra trade markers?" The alien caressed two metal contacts with the long thumb of each hand. Sparks leapt, and she made a hissing sound. "Ssss . . . We wander from the subject. What quarrel could any sentient being have with our decision? It is not denied that Diplomat-by-Choice Ktashisnif died in the hands of the"—she used the human word—"kidnappers."

"No."

"Three days in agony, then death, a direct result of the actions of Jackson and the three Shrenks. They sought to hide in the swarming humanity of New York City. Ktashisnif was allergic to human beings, and the kidnappers had no allergy serum for her. These things are true."

"True enough. But our courts wouldn't have charged them with murder by slow torture." In fact, a good lawyer might have gotten them off by arguing that a Chirpsithra wasn't human before the law. I didn't say so. I said, "Jackson and the Shrenk brothers probably didn't know about Chirpsithra allergies."

"There are no accidents during the commission of a crime. Be reasonable. Next you will say that one who kills the wrong victim during an attempt at murder may claim that the death was an accident, that she should be set free to try again."

"I am reasonable. All I want is for all this to blow over so that I can open the Draco Tavern again." I sipped at the whiskey. "But there's no point in that until I can get some customers again. I wish you had let the bastards plead guilty to a lesser sentence. For that matter, I wish you hadn't invited reporters in to witness the executions."

She was disturbed now. "But such was your right, by ancient custom! Rick Schumann, are you not reassured to know that we did not inflict more pain on the criminals than they inflicted on Ktashisnif?"

For three days the world had watched while Chirpsithra executioners smothered four men slowly to death. In some nations it had even been televised.

"It was terrible publicity. Don't you see, we don't do things like that. We've got laws against cruel and unusual punishment."

"How do you deal with cruel and unusual crimes?"

I shrugged.

"Cruel and unusual crimes require cruel and unusual punishment. You humans lack a sense of proportion, Rick Schumann. Drink more whiskey?"

She brushed her thumbs across the contacts and made a hissing sound. I drank more whiskey. Maybe it would improve my sense of proportion. It was going to be a long time before I opened the Draco Tavern again.

THE ONES WHO STAY HOME

P assengers from *Wandering Signal* had come to the Draco Tavern in my hour of need. I thanked them for that, and I set about serving them.

Somewhere in the wreckage of the bar was a bag that looked like bird kibble. Blue Bubble would eat that, but there wasn't any point in looking. In this disorder I couldn't identify it. Too much of what I keep for my alien clientele looks like bags of kibble.

The Boojum would take salt water, a careful balance that didn't match Earth's oceans. I keep a jar of salts, and for a wonder, I found it. I mixed it with water—the tap was still running—and got the Boojum to test it for proportions.

The Chirpsithra need sparkers. Those I found. My wall sockets weren't delivering power. I was relieved to see the Chirps had brought a power pack.

Sissy didn't need anything.

I needed painkillers and an alcohol-free beer. We took it all to one of the intact booths. I had to let the Boojum do the carrying. None of my staff was present—Tony was still in the hospital—and I was still healing.

The bar, the Tavern's central pit, had taken most of the damage. Various force fields damped some of the blast. Most of the booths were intact, and a few still had float chairs and privacy fields. I picked a float chair to put me at conversation level with the Chirps.

"Yes, we fight," I said, continuing a discussion. "In most mammal species the males duel for mating privileges or property rights. We humans still do a little of that. Hey, even caterpillars fight for territory. It's universal."

"That gives no mapping for what happened here," Blue Bubble grumbled, "this lethal vandalism." Blue Bubble was as big as our large airlock, and I couldn't tell what was inside it.

Sissy was an energy pattern who lived in a bell jar of thin ionized plasma. Her native habitat was at the rarefied edge of a gas giant planet's atmosphere. Her life processes gave out a thin, wavering hiss. She spoke through a standard translator. "In the archaic state of nature," she said, "we might wrestle to overwhelm each other's magnetic patterns. We do this to gain dominance within a vortex. Victor superimposes its memory on the loser. It is not normal to die in battle, but it can happen, patterns merge and conflict, a flare, both gone."

"Then you don't have a problem with terrorists?"

"A tale out of history," Sissy said to me. "Wesshenss Bondbreaker's family vortex built an iron kite and ran it into a stratospheric storm. The tail he guided into a meeting of the Guidance Vortex. Half the Guidance was blown out. Wesshenss disrupted too. Would you call Wesshenss a terror maker?"

I said, "Not unless he was trying to frighten someone. Wesshenss was trying to *kill* the Guidance, wasn't he?"

"Yes. I don't understand this term, 'terror.'"

"Extreme fear," I said. "It isn't what one can do to an enemy, it's what one can make an enemy do to itself. If one can put an enemy country—political entity, culture, whatever—in a state of terror, the enemy may do crazy things."

"It's not a useful term," one of the Chirpsithra said. The two looked identical—slender lobsters eleven feet tall—and I didn't try to tell them apart.

Blue Bubble said, "When we fear an enemy, we fight him. Why would any entity want us to fear him?"

"Among us there is doubt as to what is a person," Sissy said. "Attacker and defender may merge or trade packets of information. One may become the other. Your Golden Rule is mere common sense to us."

The Boojum said nothing.

"Terrorist is not for us a useful term. You must understand," one of the Chirpsithra said, "that no entity would achieve interstellar flight if extreme forms of vandalism were a problem. The energies involved are too great. The power in *Wandering Signal* would shatter most habitats. Planets, for instance."

"What do you do about vandals?" I asked.

"Many things. Our greatest threat is from the dead universe, from kinetic energy, from impacts large or tiny. Most tool users cannot match the fury of a meteor impact or a blast of cosmic rays. We make the ship self-repairing. We blast small intersecting masses and steer around large ones. These same defenses would repel many potential enemies."

"Design flaws," the other Chirp said. "Things go wrong with any machine or system. We build to resist accidental damage. Thus the ship will also resist imposed damage, sabotage."

"We don't land the mother ship," Chirp One said. "*Wandering Signal* now orbits the Earth's Moon. Wherever entities probe the universe more deeply than you have, we still leave *Wandering Signal* out of easy reach."

Chirp Two leaned toward me. "Rick, your people say 'terrorist' and 'freedom fighter' and 'soldier,' 'espionage' and 'murder' and 'homicide,' as if you must know an enemy's motive. You deal with only one species. It must be easy to predict what people of your own kind will do. But we deal with a myriad kinds of intelligence.

"More than that, there are deviants. Few species evolve toward the conditions of interstellar travel, therefore it is deviants who board our ships. We must be very wary of our own passengers. Even ourselves, even crew may go mad.

"So, our concern is not with who might try to damage us, or why. Some of you use another term, 'threat estimate.' For every creature or hive or plausible grouping, there is a threat estimate. How much damage could it do to us? How shall we protect against it?"

"That sounds insanely complicated," I said.

"Intrusive," said the Blue Bubble. "We were probed down to our atomic structure before we were allowed to board. We entered *Wandering Signal* naked, and found life support inside. All are so treated. What the crew learns is useful for medical treatment, so we are told."

"That sounds likely," I said.

"Objection!" Blue Bubble said. "Medical repairs interfere with our ongoing evolution! What if we refuse the probes?"

"Stay home," one Chirp said.

"To stay home is easy," the other said. "Stay within the bounds of one's evolution. Stay where dangers are known. Most sapient species can't travel. They would need life support so extensive that they could not perceive the universe beyond. Information flow is so easy. Why do we go?"

I asked, "Why did you?"

She didn't answer. I looked to the Boojum, who said, "I was made, an elaborate multisensual camera. I was to carry sensations home to my makers, who were not able to leave their swamp. The swamps dried despite all efforts. To stay home is only relatively safe. May I show you some of the wonders I have collected?"

I said, "My systems are down."

"But the danger to *Wandering Signal* suggests its own solution," the Blue Bubble said. "Why not bar everybody? Why not explore as the Boojum's people do . . . did?"

I thought: why doesn't Congress shut down all airports?

The Chirp said, "Knowledge. All this mingling of near-infinite varying viewpoints is certain to produce new tools, ideas, techniques, philosophies, art. Whether these things are worth the risks is a judgment call. A tiny few of us choose to travel. Ten-to-the-fourteenth Chirpsithra stay home, those who see risks as greater than rewards."

Blue Bubble said, "Yet you claim all red dwarf stars."

"Only travelers settle other worlds, mate and breed. Most Chirpsithra descend from travelers. Most of every species worth talking to descends from travelers."

I said, "Robert Heinlein once wrote that you do not truly own anything that you can't carry in both arms at a dead run."

"Yet you stay home, Rick Schumann," said one of the Chirps.

"And look what that got me."

"You will rebuild. Somewhere among your population are the vandals who attacked the Draco Tavern. They will be brought to our justice. We have set Folk in charge of finding them. Half our passenger complement is playing the detective game, enjoying themselves greatly, building or borrowing forensic techniques—"

Like a role-playing game, I thought. Wait, now— "The Folk?"

"Who better?"

The Folk are hunters. They don't eat unless there is prey to track down.

The thought gave me a moment's vicious pleasure. Then I asked, "What if there are a lot of terrorists involved?"

"The law is already established. One of us died in the explosion. They belong to our justice. Why would numbers matter?"

Whole nations had backed the killers who brought down the World Trade Center. The bomber who attacked the Draco Tavern might represent a political party, a nation, a religious movement, or—it was not beyond possibility that a whole world could be held responsible.

I said, "A sense of proportion can be a valuable thing."

Trucks were pulling up outside. These must be the repair crews I'd asked for, though of course they'd have to get through our security. "I'd best deal with this," I said.

One of the Chirps said, "Vandals of a species now deceased once destroyed a planet housing four times ten-to-the-ninth of our kind. What sense of proportion should we have shown then? Would it matter that most of us escaped?"

But men in hard hats were waving at me, and I went to answer them.

BREEDING MAZE

The Draco Tavern can be hot and cold, wet and dry, the air compressed or rarefied and of varying composition. Booth-sized temperature zones inside the dome must serve an eerie variety of alien visitors. But outside the Tavern, the Mount Forel environment is thin and frozen, the vegetation sparse and hardy.

We use the cold in various ways. Storage for an unearthly variety of perishables is behind the Tavern, along with a wide range of toilet facilities.

But we use the Tavern's facilities too. Housing for me and my staff is a wing of the Tavern, and the climate control is the best on Earth. We don't get colds or allergies. Working the Draco Tavern isn't for everyone—it can freak you out, and some of my staff have stayed only hours—but it has its compensations.

One of last night's animals came in loose. I looked around for its owner and didn't see him.

As it stalked toward the bar from one of the small airlocks, I watched uneasily. Who might help with this? There hadn't been any Chirpsithra in the Draco Tavern last night, and there weren't any now. Rory was watching too, but he was across the room serving customers. The customers didn't seem disturbed, but it's not easy reading alien body language.

The beast would mass around a hundred and thirty pounds. It was hairy and musky. It walked as a biped: two short hind legs, four short, powerful-looking arms, and a mouth not quite like any mammal's, but not insectoid. I'd looked for teeth last night, but seen none. I couldn't guess what it might eat.

It moved up against the bar, close enough that I could smell doggy breath, and suddenly reached over. I shied back. It snatched up a loose translator and snarled at it. The translator spoke.

I reached for my stun, and then the sense of the words reached me. "Was I stupid last night?"

I said, "Stupid? You were—" and stopped, feeling very foolish. "Yeah."

"Did anything bad happen?"

"Two of you came in with one of the spindly aliens, a Joker. He had you both on a leash, a tether. We don't allow pets in the Draco Tavern, but I wasn't quite ready to raise the point, because none of the crew were in." The crews of the interstellar liners are all Chirpsithra, and they're more or less in charge. "I thought it was their business, not mine, long as you stayed leashed. Also, I wondered which of you was the pet. In here you can't always tell."

"I comprehend."

"The Joker brought you up to the bar and started talking. Talking fast." It was starting to dawn on me that I'd been played for a fool. "And one of you voided something smelly against the bar."

"Sorry."

"The automatics got it. The Joker told me the two of you had been thawed by accident. Pets and children travel frozen, right? That's if the liners will have them at all. But you were pets and you'd been thawed, and you had to be kept exercised until . . . it sounded like legal problems."

"Jokers are well known as practical jokers," the beast said.

Given the species name, you wouldn't think I'd need to be told that. But the Joker was a tall, spindly creature with dead-white skin partly covered with green hair or moss, and a triangular, somewhat manlike face with a jutting jaw and a permanent grin. I'd thought, *Batman reference,* and my brain stopped working. No alien would have thought to warn me of *that.*

I'd got to talking to the Joker. He sounded like someone dancing on a bagful of walnuts, a rattling sound, but his translator took care of that. He seemed intelligent, interested. I told him about running the Tavern. He talked freely, it seemed, about his own background and species. A hotter star than Sol, a planet with a longer year, cultivated land losing fertility. . . . His pets were a little whiny and not quite housebroken—

I asked, "Were you drugged?"

"No, not drugged. We are Pazensh. We grow intelligence when we come into heat."

"Really?"

"Yes, we need intelligence to seek and find and test a mate. At other times we survive on reflexes and paranoia. You—?"

"With us it's pretty much the other way around," I said. I had no mate right now; Jehaneh was visiting family in Iraq. "And you chewed up a stool. The Joker paid for that, but the Bebebebeque on the stool had to leap for its life. I never knew it could do that." The big yellow bug had jumped about four meters.

The Pazensh said, "I remember not quite enough about last night, but it ended with a whiff of female scent, and a door that closed and locked. It took me some time to gather my wits, and more to solve the lock and get out of the lander. Then I followed her scent here. Here I find my own scent, and scents of many species, and now I must ask how badly I've embarrassed myself."

"Nothing we can't handle," I said. "I've done this dance before. Let's see, you didn't use the restrooms, but that happens with other species too. They can be complicated. The little bug's okay—" and it wouldn't matter much if the Bebebebeque had been eaten; they're a hive species. "All's clear."

"Good. Now I must find my mate." The Pazensh started to climb over the bar.

"Hold up." I showed him the stun. "What are you doing?"

He stopped. "Following a scent trail."

"One of your females is back behind my bar?"

"Is or was." The Pazensh settled onto a stool. His many-toed feet dangled; the long toes thrummed with his eagerness. "Name me Hass. My companion, my will-be-darling, she is Tenshir. You?"

"Rick."

"If we were more than one female and one male, I would smell it. Tenshir is using your establishment as a—"The translator hiccoughed, then said, "breeding maze."

I said, "Hass, we have laws to block your mating against your partner's will."

"When I have found Tenshir, you may ask her wishes. For now, she must test my intelligence."

"You're following a scent trail of pheromones. That's intelligence?"

His toes stopped moving. "That doesn't make sense, does it? Following her scent will hardly engage my mind. But she has marked the domain, the perimeter of the breeding maze. She is here and I must find her." Hass surged over the counter and down the stairs into the storerooms, running on all sixes. I followed his path with the point of the stun, but didn't fire.

If I'd seen a Chirp I'd have asked for help. There were ten varied aliens in the bar, all staring at me, most of them unfamiliar species. And Rory was at the service window. "Boss? Three silvers for the Wids, unless you're—"

"Rory, take over." I didn't like doing that. The Tavern can run a crew of up to six residents plus day help, but this year's interstellar liner was a small one with less than a dozen passengers. Miranda, on duty last night, was sleeping it off. Only Rory was on duty.

But Hass wasn't the only one getting an intelligence test here. I donned an air filter and kept the stun. I walked down the stairs slowly, giving myself time to think.

I couldn't just let Hass run loose here. My staff wears air filters when they come to the basement for drinks and edibles. It was a maze even to me, but a maze of stocks for more than fifty alien varieties who had visited the tavern at various times. Most of what feeds one life-form would be poison to a score of others. Chemicals were in the air.

It was cold down here. Siberian temperatures are good for storing a lot of my stocks; others have to be chilled, heated, pressurized, or irradiated. I caught a whiff of Hass's scent, but not enough to guide me. I followed a scuffling.

"Hass," I called, "how long is this likely to take?"

"A breeding maze? There is no telling. Hours or days, perhaps."

"Are you allowed to get help with this?"

Still unseen, Hass answered. "Any may help. This is a mating maze, not—" The translator hiccoughed. "—an entertainment. The stakes are the highest. If I can trust a companion, it speaks for my intelligence. If I choose one who will mock me, or a fool who will lead me astray, that speaks too."

"Okay."

"Rick, is the Draco Tavern a successful concern?"

I chuckled. "Yes." *My* intelligence test.

"Good. I trace your scent and hers, and several other human and Chirpsithra. Does that match—"

"Chirpsithra come down here, sure. All my staff are human."

"And a Joker was here."

I'd been thinking about the Joker. Given what I knew now, he'd learned more last night than I was comfortable with. Time I found out something about him. I used my translator to call *Shock Layer,* the Chirpsithra liner currently hovering near the Earth's Moon.

I got an answering device. "I'll talk to any member of the crew," I told it.

"Hi, Rick. The crew are dealing with internal matters. You have not clearance."

"Search the passenger lists for Jokers." I spelled it in the Chirp language, as best I could.

"Joker. One passenger, Hsenshesist Brill, adult male, restricted to ship."

"Hsenshesist is on Earth," I said.

"That information is restricted." Pause. "I have upgraded your clearance. Hsenshesist Brill has gone missing. Where is he now and what is he doing?"

"He's in the vicinity of the Draco Tavern. He's running a scheme of some kind. What are his capabilities?"

"It was not expected that he could board the lander. He is barred from Earth. We must upgrade his capability estimates. Keep me informed," the mechanism said.

I disconnected. I whispered to my translator to get a hologram map of the cellar. A skittering told me Hass was running above me along the stacks of boxes, left, down, left again and up and back toward me. I broke into a jog, the hologram glowing ahead of me like a complex flashlight beam.

"Your help has been of little use," Hass said. He was over my head.

"Slow down."

"Tenshir will not slow!"

"She'll be faster than you. You have to stop to sniff. You'll never catch up unless you guess where she'll be. How would she break a scent trail? Can she fly?"

"No, not without an aircraft or lift belt. We do not use mechanical aids for this, barring what our hands can make. You see me naked, yes? She will be too."

"Can she jump long gaps?"

"She might make four meters. I would still scent her."

"Will she have help?"

"Hsenshesist Brill must have thawed us at the same time. The med system that held us was in the lander, and the scent led here. Snowfall might have disturbed the scent trail. Who would we meet on the path to the Draco Tavern? You," he answered himself: the obvious suspect. "And a female human server. Has Tenshir approached you?"

"No. And it's Jennifer's sleep cycle, and you didn't come near her last night."

A long, low, modulated snarl. The translator said, "Did Tenshir speak to you of a stalker with rape in mind? And beg help?"

I repeated, "No."

"Last night, who else did we approach?"

"Things have been pretty dead this trip. There were only seven or eight customers last night, all at one table. Brill and his pets tried to join them, but they got yelled at."

"Do you think she's alone, then? Rick!" His voice dropped as if she might be in earshot. "The toilets!"

"Right. Here, these steps lead out."

I store some stocks outside in the Siberian cold. Animals won't come near the weirder chemicals, and the temperature stays low enough. Housing for human staff forms an arc partway around the dome. The toilets are outside too, completing more of the arc.

Hass dashed ahead of me.

"Humans have a poor sense of smell," I said.

"How I envy you." But Hass's spongy tip of a nose was in the air. "Like a chemistry lab. These two booths are for Chirpsithra. This for several types; a Joker has used it. This one I could use, or Tenshir." He sniffed. "Tenshir has not used it. Some Tiktik have."

"How long can she hold her wastes?"

Hass spoke; the translator said, "Two days or longer." A sudden yip. "Rick! The ceiling!"

In the booth that a Pazensh might use, I looked up at an alien pictograph: a hundred tiny symbols arrayed in a near-ellipse. I said, "She didn't use this booth except as a drop."

"She got in ahead of the Tiktik and hoped their smell would cover hers. My mate is clever."

"What's it say?"

" 'When zeeft fayristtent waves . . . it's a puzzle. It won't work in your speech."

While he worked on the puzzle, I called *Shock Layer* again. "How often does a Joker need a toilet? Which toilet would he use?"

The answering device said, "A Joker must void liquid wastes once every three hours or so. Stony solids, up to ten standard days. Gullet stones, every five hundred days. Number hash mub delta." Fourth booth to my right. "Have you data for me, Rick?"

"He's been here. What motivates a Joker? Why did this one board a Chirp ship, and why did they let him on?"

"Hsenshesist Brill is a famous xenopsychologist. Ship law restricts him because he runs uncomfortable experiments on sapient entities, but his lectures rank high. Many will attend when he tells us what he has done on your world."

"What will he do? Knock down a building? Nuke a city and study the survivors?"

"He will do nothing harmful. Deaths would place him in a new category, outside the protection of citizenship. Hsenshesist Brill is not deemed mad."

"Good." What then? Would he start a career as an alien rock star and study the groupies? Go into politics? Crash the stock market? Smuggle something alien, like Glig medicines?

"Liquid wastes?" I asked, "Are they easy to track?"

"I have specs for your local toilets. He could use those."

Dammit. I disconnected. "Hass?"

"The puzzle is incomplete," Hass said. "It's as if she stopped when almost finished. Why would she do that?"

"Drew the rest of it elsewhere." The ellipse of markings had a bite missing. "Fits here." I looked hard at the oddly configured bowl that was the centerpiece of the cubicle. Detergent spray from here, warm air from here, two-stage flush, outlet underneath. It was in my mind that if I wanted to hide a puzzle from a human woman, I'd draw it on the bottom of a toilet seat . . . but I couldn't see anything analogous here.

The puzzle had me in thrall. I went outside. Piled snow allowed me to crawl onto the roof. The roof was covered with packed ice, and no patterns had been carved into it.

Hass wouldn't carry a heater—no store-bought tools—but he might make a scraper to get through this ice sheet to reveal a message. "Hass? You've been telling me she wants to be caught. We're not looking for anything terribly difficult. Hass?"

Nothing. I got off the roof and looked into the cubicle. The Pazensh was gone.

So the question was, Did I want to lead Hass to Tenshir? We weren't looking for the same thing. Puzzle aside, it wasn't my species' problem. Further—despite the appearance that she'd left a message, it was still possible that Hass was a stalker.

What I wanted was to find the Joker. Whatever devilment Brill was planning on Earth, he'd played me for a fool last night.

He could use a men's room, or a ladies', but he couldn't pass for human. Where could he hide, and still accomplish anything?

We sometimes use pressure suits for a cleanup. I went back in and put one on. Now a Joker couldn't smell me. I went back to the appropriate toilet, hash mub delta, and set a tiny security camera.

He'd need food . . . but the age of terrorism has not quite faded. There were already cameras in the Tavern's food preparation area.

It couldn't be this straightforward. Think of something else.

I hadn't needed to call *Shock Layer.* All of my possible customers are in my registry before they ever reach the Tavern . . . but Brill wasn't supposed to have come here at all. Hmm? I used the translator to look him up, and there he was.

Physiologically and chemically, Brill was a tee tee arrowhead slant ool, which meant he'd have to carry supplements: pills or a needle. Otherwise he could get what he wanted at any market. Of course any market clerk would see him for an alien. He wouldn't be too conspicuous if he stayed in the Mount Forel Spaceport area, unless someone called the cops. Me or any Chirpsithra officer. Could he risk that?

Aliens did often possess special, valuable knowledge. If Brill left the Mount Forel area, he might persuade someone that he had, say, the secret of immortality. Hell, it might be true: he might have got it from a Glig. So someone outside might hide him—

But what did he want with the Pazensh?

For the first time I wondered if Brill might have taken the Pazensh female. (For what?) And left Hass behind. (Why?) But if there were a scheme involving the Pazensh, he'd have to hang around. (Where?)

Actually—to a Joker, that might have an answer.

I stripped off my pressure suit behind the bar. "Rory? How's it go?"

"Rick, the Wids want to try sparkers. Shall I? I thought sparkers were just for Chirpsithra."

"Sure, and alcohol is just for humans, but a lot of aliens want to try liqueurs. I always, always check their registry." I reset the translator. "There. Wids are ahn tee hatch nex zep. It won't injure them." They wouldn't like it, though.

He took a couple of sparkers and went, and noticed I was following him. Under a sound suppressor I stopped him. "Rory, you weren't in last night. There was a Joker name of Brill. It's a fugitive."

"Isn't that up to the Chirps?"

"If I'm right, it's our problem too. I'm going back to my room. If anything more goes wrong, call *Shock Layer*. This is what you tell them . . ."

Rooms for the staff are roomy enough, and the communal complex includes a pool, some exercise equipment, stuff you'd expect at a mid-level hotel. There's also quite a lot of security stuff. Staff knows and accepts that I can use a screen in my room to spy on them to a certain extent. Brill would not.

Brill had learned that most of the staff complex was empty. Of course he could be hiding on the endless miles of tundra; but where was the humor in that? And Jokers like it warm. Hiding in the staff complex would be a fine joke on me.

Where? Another species might have chosen the pool or spa.

He might have captured Miranda and taken her room, if he thought she might stumble across him.

I'd told Brill about Jehaneh. My bet was that he was in her room: my own mate's room.

I hesitated outside the door to my apartment, stun in hand. Opened the door and, for an instant, froze. Another Pazensh was there, partly embedded in something like lime Jell-O. Tenshir wriggled, and I swung left and right with my stun held high, and Brill's stun got me first.

I was still standing up, stun held high, every muscle rigid in spasm. I concentrated on breathing. It was too slow.

The spindly green-and-white Joker eeled out from under my breakfast table and looked me over. The grin didn't change, and he didn't laugh. He stepped toward my door and I heard it close and lock. Something flew past my ear. I heard two solid impacts, one as it hit, one as he fell.

Hass ran past me. I heard another thud, and more. If Hass could have used my stun, Brill would have been a lot better off.

Locked in a full-body cramp, I listened to the lovers talking.

Hass asked, "Do you know a way to get this stuff off you?"

"Only one way. Think of it as the last test."

"The tavern tender must have left word that he would search here. He's certainly that bright. In an irritatingly long time some Chirpsithra will arrive to free us and reclaim the Joker."

"That's my best answer too. Dear, how did you find me, with the puzzle incomplete and myself in the wrong place?"

"First I looked for the rest of the clue, but nothing was there. I thought, it must be that you were interrupted. We met none but two humans and the Joker last night. Jokers are notorious. Leaving me a broken and empty breeding maze would be a hoot.

"Rick Schumann was hunting the Joker. I can't use any tool I don't make myself, but Rick can. I followed Rick. His scent trail disappeared when he put on a pressure suit, so I had to work out where he'd take such a thing and follow him by eye."

"You let this local do your tracking for you?"

"I did."

"Darling, that's brilliant!"

"He spoke of the staff housing. I found the Joker's scent there. I found a broken lock. I went through to the pool, then a complex of rooms with Rick's scent and a female's. I lurked with a water flask in hand until Rick provided a distraction."

"Nice toss."

"Thank you."

"I had such a nice puzzle laid out for you. There was so much more. Did you find the sticks?"

"No, I went straight to the toilets."

"Look them up later."

"I wish I could break you loose from the police goop."

"Minor foreplay?"

I hadn't thought other life-forms were as versatile in their petting as humans. Things were getting interesting when the door behind me was blasted open and two identical Chirpsithra came in. One sprayed me in the face with something acerbic. Gradually my frozen muscles relaxed. The other set some humming thing against the green jell, and that melted away from Tenshir.

They put the Joker on a float plate and one Chirp took him away. The other stayed. I thought she would question me; but she did it her way. She led me back into the bar, leaving the Pazensh to use my rooms as they saw fit. She got me to sit down at the biggest table, me with an Irish coffee and her with a sparker, and I told the tale to every entity in the Tavern.

PLAYHOUSE

DAY ZERO

ong View reached lunar orbit as so many Chirpsithra-manned passenger ships had done before, but faster, skipping steps. There was a curtness to their negotiations with United Nations traffic control. The lander turned loose from the big ship before its orbit about the Moon was well established.

I was spending a few weeks with Jehaneh and Walt in Saddam Hussein's palace in Tikrit. The army had turned some of his old palaces into hotels back in the Twenty Zeros. Amenities were primitive and the fad had wilted, so it wasn't that expensive, considering. Saddam had had lots of interesting playground equipment . . . for adults, of course, but Walt was having a good time too.

Then the liner hove into view near the Moon and I was called back. I left Walt and Jehaneh there. The Draco Tavern was no place for a two-and-a-half-year-old boy.

DAY ONE

I got there ahead of my crew.

Reworking the Draco Tavern to accommodate new species takes preparation. I spent a few hours looking around the Tavern, then called the ship to learn what kind of visitors to expect. I was waiting on the line, chatting with the translator device, when four Chirpsithra filed through the tall-and-narrow airlock.

Chirpsithra stand eleven feet tall. They're exoskeletal creatures, usually wearing tools and pouches and rank marks attached to their scarlet chitin shells. I've learned to recognize some of the marks. Three were ranking officers. The fourth wore a sigil I'd never seen before: a triangle with curved edges. They looked around, chattering to each other with their translators turned off.

I pointed at a sparker. *Want this?* The triangle-bearer spoke in Lottl, and I heard, "Rejected with thanks. Rick Schumann?"

"That's right."

"Proprietor of this?"

"Yes, the Draco Tavern. Welcome."

"Thank you. I am Queeblishiz, Matriarch of Lifesystem Support. We have a—" The translator hesitated. "—situation."

Running this world's only interspecies bar for nearly forty years, I've seen more "situations" than I could count. I said, "See if you can describe it."

"Our cold sleep facilities have failed."

"Oboy," I said, before my mind quite caught up. How many extra visitors—? "Just a minute. Don't most of your passengers come down anyway? The Draco Tavern is popular. So's Earth."

"Passengers, yes," Queeblishiz said.

Still speculating, I said, "You'd have to fix what's broken before you can leave. You'll play hell finding tools for spacecraft on

Earth." We'd abandoned the Moon more than forty years before the first interstellar liner showed up. "How long?"

"Perhaps forty days. We carry tools to make tools."

That didn't sound bad. But the other Chirp officers were still chattering at her, and she turned off her translator and chattered back. Then, "Barman, we must upgrade your facilities, particularly your defenses."

"Defenses?" Ohmygod. Sooner or later it had to happen. "What is *Long View,* a prison ship?"

"Close. Unlucky guess. *Long View* is not unusual, a typical passenger liner with cold sleep facilities for prey animals, pets, and children. These are breaking down. The ship is too small, massively too small. We'll go insane if we can't set some of our children free on Earth."

"And prey animals too? Do you plan to run hunts through my place?"

"Those we may slaughter and clone again later. We may require the owners to care for their pets, or slaughter them too. Our concerns are for the children. We have four varieties awake."

"That doesn't sound too bad," I said.

"Yes, but we must begin at once. We must childproof the Tavern."

I phoned Arlan and Genevieve and told them the situation.

Staff at the Draco Tavern are always volunteers; they're scientists come to interact with unearthly intelligences and alien disciplines. Children were not of interest. They both bowed out.

Children and pets are normally barred from the Tavern. Variety in adult tool users has always caused problems enough.

The Chirps put electronic locks on the airlocks and toilets. I worried: what if a child was locked out? Queeblishiz reassured me. The children would have bar codes tattooed on their hides. Only the appropriate locks, and toilets, would open for them . . . and they wouldn't lock with a child inside.

Hah, that lesson must be universal! Walt hasn't locked us out of a bathroom yet, but it's a basic intelligence test for grown-ups.

The first child was already down. Djil was a streamlined humanoid massing around two hundred kilos. Most of a human's features were in place, but she had lids over every-thing: eyelids, earlids, no nose, no hair, a gristly filter behind the lips, and no obvious openings that a human would cover with clothing. I pictured her as coming from a windy, sandy world.

We put her in a shirt and jeans. She didn't object.

Djil explored the Draco Tavern and watched Queeblishiz im-pose childproofing changes. I watched it all carefully. Fragile stuff out of reach or locked away. Stairs blocked with a repel field keyed to the bar codes. Odd chemicals kept out of sight and touch, and that included everything behind and beneath my bar. Most of what I serve is lethal to something.

When a party of anthropologists showed up, Djil served their drinks, then got into an intense discussion of experimental methods.

"Her parents are too big to travel," Queeblishiz said. "They can arrest the development of children for a time. Djil is nearly seventy years old by your counting. She can babysit, but she must be watched."

"Why? She sounds like an adult to all intents and purposes."

"Watch her. Tend her. Djil's brain has not reached full weight, and she is as self-centered as any child."

DAY TWO

We barred humans from the Tavern. Protests came from various directions. Sooner or later . . . but first we'd better see just how much of a problem the children were.

"There's no need to think of me as a child," Djil told me. "I'm older than you. My parents are excessively protective. They tried to stop me from leaving. We reached a compromise. I'm listed as a child, with fewer rights than a passenger."

"That's a pity," I said. "But why were you chosen to guard the younger children?"

"I'm an available sitter, and barred from roaming at will through *Long View*. The Chirpsithra are economical."

I'd still keep a watch on her. She was too big to be taken lightly.

DAY THREE

After two days of work, Matriarch Queeblishiz brought down the children.

The Rainbow Wyrms were snakes, six of them. They were caged when Queeblishiz brought them in on a heavy lift platform. When the field was switched off, they were gone too fast to be visible. For an hour they buzzed around the Tavern, bouncing off the lock fields whenever they got near the bar. They couldn't fly, but they could jump like coiled springs. They buzzed into corners and under booths, chasing down the mice.

A few minutes wore them out, and they slowed down. They were glittering orange and green, each half a man's weight, each about three meters long. You could see a fringe of little limbs growing down the ventral line. They slept a lot, usually wrapped in knots around each other. They were friendly to visitors; I could wear one wrapped around my shoulders and neck. They ate small mammals taken from another failing freezer. Visitors would have to be marked with bar codes; any rats and mice in the Tavern were on their own.

Mit, Hel, and Sesch, the Red Demons, were a meter long, exoskeletal, with spiky red armor. "They'll attack anything their own size including each other," Queeblishiz said. "I'll give them police cuffs. They won't be able to come near each other. We can give them a confined space in the Tavern."

I suggested, "Outside. You can fence out wolves."

The Chirp Matriarch accessed some beamed-in source of data. "Wolves? I think our three charges can handle such creatures. Bigger predators might be a problem. We'll confine them to a patch of tundra and watch them for as long as this warm weather lasts. We can put the Wayward Child outside too."

The Wayward Child was a filter feeder armed with gauzy wings and a tremendous vented cavern of a mouth. She needed a lift pack to fly; her world was less massive than Earth. Siberian summer wasn't exactly warm, but it was warm enough to generate immense clouds of mosquitoes. I was going to like having the Wayward Child around. As for the rest, we'd see.

DAY FIVE

Another freezer failed.

We were lucky. It held Folk puppies. Folk from previous flights had traded for hunting grounds in various parts of the world. For a few dollars more, Nevada accepted seven hunters with their fifteen progeny. The Tavern never need see the feral pups.

"—And a few hundred Bebebebeque spawn," said Queeblishiz.

"A few *hundred*?"

Queeblishiz said, "Bebebebeque spawn must be culled. We will turn them loose in the Tavern and leave the Rainbow Wyrms to deal with them."

I had long since stopped seeing signs of mice inside the Tavern, barring tiny heaps of tiny bones and tufts of fur. That was nice. I didn't like an infestation of bugs! "Why not outside? Give them more room to run."

"They like it warm," Queeblishiz said implacably.

Bebebebeque infants were the size of my thumb, little golden bugs looking a lot like their parents. For a couple of days they were all over the place, snatching food of the tee tee hatch nex ool variety, including my own meals. Hyperquick Rainbow Wyrms were all over the place, hunting them down. The bugs became scarce, then invisible. Survivors had learned to hide.

DAY NINE

Jehaneh had worked in the Tavern on and off for a year, before and a little after Walt's birth. It's a good way to study aliens. She knew the territory and she had all the passes. This time she didn't phone ahead; she just flew in.

I saw her coming through one of the bigger airlocks, dressed for Arctic cold, manipulating Walt and a lot of his gear. I went to meet her.

"Hi," she said. "If I'd phoned you'd have told me not to come."

I said, "Yes." I started moving Walt, his stroller, his toys, diapers, powder and Q-tips, food. "Where's your stuff?"

"Still in the SUV. But I got to thinking. Picture Walt in his teens, or in his thirties," her hands flat on my chest so I had to look her in the eye, "knowing that his father runs the only bar for aliens in the known universe—"

"But that's just Earth."

"—And he never got in to see it when he was a kid." Her eyes roved, seeking the newest lot of aliens.

There weren't any, barring Speedy, who looks like an abstract sculpture of a turtle and doesn't move fast enough to notice. Speedy pushed his way through the jelly lock two years ago and is on his way to a booth. The Rainbow Wyrms were hiding, and the rest of the kids were outside, even Djil. Nonetheless Jehaneh said, "This place is the most wonderful toy on Earth."

"Yes, dear, but other children are using it."

"That's—"

A whirr and a wind and a glimpse of orange-green passed between our noses. Jehaneh yelped and threw herself back. I caught her wrists so that she missed falling on Walt and hit flat floor. I was kneeling beside her in an instant.

"I'm all right," she said, and sat up, and clutched the back of her head. "What was that?"

"That was the Rainbow Wyrms. They're very fast." They'd slowed down now, but six orange-green snakes surrounded us, ready to investigate. I snatched up Walt. "I have to put a bar code on him *right now.*"

"Bar code?" She tried to follow me behind the bar. The field stopped her, so she watched while I peeled down Walt's shorts and stamped his butt. The mark was a simplified picture of a set of alien fangs.

"It keeps the others away from him." Keeps him from being eaten, I didn't say. "The tracers can read the mark through clothing. Show me some skin, woman."

She didn't argue: she bared enough of her butt for a flu shot. I stamped her.

"Rick, did you mean actual children?"

I started to explain. Djil had come in through the big lock, and I waved at her awesome pink bulk. "That's Djil. She's old enough to babysit. Djil, this is Jehaneh."

"The Red Demons are loose," Djil said.

"*Loose?* How loose?"

"Barman, I only turned my back for a time-hack. The sky was full of birds. The Wayward Child tried to catch one. You know, she shouldn't do that. These birds are much too big for her mouth, but there aren't any big birds where she comes from, and while I was turning around the bird wriggled loose and dove down over the Red Demons and it hit the origin point of the field, the singularity." She waved her arms. "Flash! And the first thing the Demons did was try to get *me*! I got to the airlock—"

"Good. Don't go out there. Jehaneh, don't go outside."

Djil said, "The toilets are all around the back."

Not true. There was a bathroom for humans in my quarters, but all the alien sanitation equipment— "We'll find you a bucket. Are you all right?" The smell had just reached me: Djil was scorched across the back of her clothing.

"I am not hurt."

"I'd better call the ship."

One of the Red Demons was trying to batter its way to me through the Tavern's glass wall. Though half my height, he looked spiky and devilish. I couldn't see the others. That bothered me.

The translator said, "Rick, hello."

"Get me Queeblishiz or any crewperson connected with children."

Matriarch Queeblishiz came on. "Barman, your call is opportune. Another freezer has failed. The lander is here boarding—"

"The Red Demons are loose. Your confinement field failed."

"Details."

I described the situation. The Red Demon was still watching me through the glass. "I've lost track of two of them. Djil, what were you doing out there?"

"Feeding them, barman, but they didn't come. They wanted the birds. See, I dropped their food at the airlock."

Yes, I could see the cage and the red-furred prey inside. "Queeblishiz, they're hungry. They'll be outside chasing ducks. They'll still be wearing police cuffs if you can activate them. Can you track them?"

"If they're on the tundra, we can stun them from orbit, once the lander is in place. Keep them occupied." She clicked off.

Djil said, "Don't do anything to hurt the Red Demons."

"No." You didn't harm children, if that's what they were. Worse yet—but call them children. The one I could see was under an overhung roof. It stopped clawing at the glass, made a rude gesture, and went around the curve and out of sight.

The lander was near the Moon. We wouldn't get help from the Chirpsithra for many hours.

A bit of a search found the other Red Demons. All three were now wandering around the line of airlocks. One found a way to open the cage. They ate the prey animals, messily, then continued to explore the locks.

I hadn't been thinking in terms of escape until now. No problem: we could get out through the bar, downstairs and through the storerooms under the Tavern. But it was safer in the Tavern.

Then one of the Demons figured out the small airlock.

"Behind the bar," I ordered, and looked around and didn't see Walt.

Djil," I snapped, "get into the bar." I didn't want to worry about her too. Walt at two and a half was surprisingly agile. When he saw he was being chased he chugged off between and around booths, under float chairs, around the bar and off again.

Jehaneh and I tried to corner him.

It wasn't that easy. The Draco Tavern has been a dome for most of its life. There weren't any corners, and there were plenty of obstacles for adults. Another problem was that Djil hadn't obeyed: she too was trying to corner Walt.

I think Walt found her scary. She was too big. He tried to climb the ladder to the loft. The field repelled him, and he dashed around a booth and was lost to us.

The Red Demon who had figured out the lock got inside, then looked around, undecided. The Rainbow Wyrms buzzed around us, bouncing off the fields. Walt charged at the Demon from around a booth, then stopped, startled. They looked at each other, then at Jehaneh and me easing toward them. Another Demon was coming through the small lock. Where was Djil?

Djil came up from the storage space under the bar. She was carrying four cages occupied by furry red creatures from another star. She opened the cages and shook the creatures out onto the floor.

The third Demon stopped just inside the lock, confronted by a lot of motion. He decided: he scrambled toward a sudden cluster of golden bugs. Something snapped, and he howled.

"They mustn't be hurt!" Djil cried. "Can't you see? They're the Chirpsithra males!"

Well, yes, I'd seen the resemblance. The Chirpsithra never talk about their sex lives, and nobody's ever seen one pregnant, and sexual dimorphism isn't uncommon even on Earth. *Sure,* they could be carrying their mates in cold sleep.

The poor bastard was wriggling like he'd stepped into a bear trap. I couldn't see what had him; but it wasn't my doing. I guessed that the tiny Bebebebeque were setting traps. We'd better stay clear of them.

Walt cooed and tried to reach the Demon. The field held them apart. An airborne snake ricocheted off the Demon, then Walt, not attacking, just using the repulsive fields to play with momentum.

"Jehaneh," I said, "get behind the bar. Watch your footing."

"I have to get Walt."

"Walt, follow your mother. Jehaneh, the fields won't let you pick him up out here. They don't work inside the bar. Walt!"

But Walt was playing with the snakes. When I tried to get to him, I stepped into something that snapped shut on my toe.

It didn't quite cut through my shoe. I wrestled my way out of it, noting the tiny components of a trap, noting also the Rainbow Wyrm wriggling out of another. Two Red Demons freed the third. I got behind Walt and shooed him toward the bar.

DAY TEN

The lander came down eleven hours after I'd called for help. They hadn't found anything from the air, barring the Wayward Child, who had wandered several kilometers in search of bigger and better clouds of mosquitoes.

Queeblishiz came out surrounded by eleven Bebebebeque. They were normal size, the size of a fifth of Haig Pinch and somewhat the same shape. A massive yellow-and-purple snake followed them, a score of skinny arms folded along its belly. What followed the snake looked like a polar bear in a fur suit: the head was conspicuously large, with a shortened snout, and a pair of darker fur lapels ran down her snowy-white fur torso.

They made their ways through various airlocks.

The Red Demons, Walt, Jehaneh, and the five remaining Rainbow Wyrms were playing together, all separated by the fields. I saw Walt pounce on something small and furry, look it over, then toss it two-handed to one of the snakes.

The little snakes came at the big snake's whistle. I don't know what the Bebebebeque did, but a score of little bugs crawled out from somewhere and ran into the ring of big Bebebebeque.

So it was nearly over, and I wasn't sure how to feel about that.

I told Queeblishiz, "The kids can't get to each other, but that doesn't mean they can't play with each other. It's been like an invisible zoo. They like it. Walt dashed out there while we weren't looking. Djil turned the prey animals loose, and they've all been scampering around catching them, even Walt."

"I take it we still cannot invite visitors here."

"I'd say no. Look at the place, it's infested! But we're recording everything. We'll have videotape to sell. How are your repairs going?"

"We'll have a cold sleep locker in two days. Which of the children would you like to be rid of first?"

I thought. "It's getting colder. I wouldn't want to bring the Wayward Child inside. Better take her."

"Not these? Not the Red Demons?"

"We seem to have struck a balance. Just reassure me that the fields will hold."

"The fields will hold, and so will the police cuffs on the Demons. Also, you will have parents. We have persuaded them to tend their children until more tanks are available. My apology, Rick, that should have happened earlier. Our passengers are explorers; they may neglect their duties.

"Of course there are none to supervise Djil or the Wayward

Child. Djil wants entertainment. We brought down a virtual set for her. The Wayward Child is harmless; let her roam free. The Bebebe-beque have finished their culling and will go back to the ship with their clan. I will stay to guard the Red Demons."

"One got injured."

"I see that. They heal fast."

"We lost a Wyrm too, to the traps. Who is the bulky individual?"

"Harharharish, come and meet the barman. Rick, she has been in cold sleep with her brood—"

Harharharish opened her lapels. Seven on each side, nestled in two vertical runnels, her brood clung to folds of skin and suckled. They looked like miniatures of their mother.

"She isn't sapient while she suckles, but that time is nearly over. Tomorrow the children will be all over the Tavern and Harharharish will begin their education. Give me the bar code marker, Rick, before all chaos breaks loose."

DAY THIRTY-ONE

Her brood surrounded her in a ring. Harharharish was reading to them, in English. Walt was among them, listening quietly.

The Wayward Child was inside, hovering near the top of the dome. She wasn't happy. I couldn't help that. A blizzard was raging beyond the dome.

Queeblishiz spoke, and I jumped, because she wasn't in the Tavern. "Rick, the lander is down. We will take the children aboard as soon as your climate is habitable again. How long will that be?"

"I never know how long a blizzard will last," I said.

Pause. "We'll send a tank."

Oh, yeah? "You carry a tank big enough for the Wayward Child?"

Pause. Hell, she must be in orbit around the Moon, not on

the lander. "We'll generate it. One hour. Rick, this affair must have cut deep into your profits. We will pay recompense."

"That's fine."

Two-point-four seconds passed. "I would have come to bid you good-bye, but I cannot tolerate your environment."

"Are you all right?"

"We're all pregnant."

The impulse to laugh disappeared in an instant. "What are Chirpsithra children like?"

"Voracious," Queeblishiz said. "Good-bye."

Jehaneh handed me an Irish coffee, half strength. "I'm going to miss them," she said.

"Which?"

"Well . . . the mother bear. The rest I can do without, except that Walt loved the snakes. Djil, where do you go from here?"

Djil said, "Colorado. The Folk are planning a Grand Canyon run, puppies and all. They'll go home on the next ship. Where do you go?"

Jehaneh looked the question at me. I said, "From this point on the Tavern is for adults, unless it's adults and Walt. You've played barmaid here. You think Walt is safe?"

She thought it over. She said, "Yeah."

LOST

Two United Nations personnel were waiting for me when I wobbled off Vanayn's dinghy. Vanayn looked at them, then brushed past. They stepped out of his path. He massed around three hundred kilos, and within the bubble helmet his mouth was a horrorshow of blades.

The tall one, a nordik-looking woman, forced a handful of papers on me. "You're Rick Schumann? Proprietor of the Draco Tavern?"

"Lucky guess." I took the papers without looking.

"I'm Dr. Cheri Kaylor. This is Carlos Magliocco," a dumpy Mediterranean-looking guy. "We need to interview you, debrief you, before you forget anything. May we—?"

My mind was one long fog bank. I said, "The Tavern."

She looked at me doubtfully. Then she took my arm before I fell over.

The dumpy man drove us down in an SUV. He didn't say much. We entered the Tavern through one of the big airlocks.

The Tavern was unchanged. Intellectually I'd expected that. Emotionally, I was just starting to resume my life. Nothing was broken, nothing added, nothing vanished. The customers were the same I'd left behind, a few missing, a few added. Vanayn was chattering with some Chirpsithra at the big table.

David Cho, whom I'd left waiting tables, came to greet me. "How was the ride?" he asked.

I shook my head. "Feed me."

"What do you want?"

"Doesn't matter."

Dr. Kaylor said, "Mr. Schumann—"

"We can talk while we eat," I said. "You want anything?"

"All right." She looked at her companion and asked, "Nachos?" Looked at me, took my arm again, and got me settled in a booth. "You could use a drink, Mr. Schumann."

"Yeah. David? Tea." My hands trembled.

Kaylor said, "That must have been quite a ride."

I smiled. I hadn't smiled in some time. "You might say so."

"You've only been gone seven hours."

"Really? When did they send for you, Dr. Kaylor?"

"Mr. Cho phoned us before you reached the airlock, he says. We've been waiting in the Tavern. This place is a wild experience, Mr. Schumann."

"The Tavern? I've gotten used to it over the years," I said. Thirty-two years now since I founded the Draco Tavern. Thirty-four since the first of the Chirpsithra interstellar liners took up orbit around the Moon, and the bubble shapes of the landers floated down the Earth's magnetic lines to Mount Forel in Siberia.

Spaghetti arrived. I began to eat, but slowly. It was a good choice, but I wasn't used to it.

She asked, "How did it happen? Nobody else has ever been offered this privilege."

I shrugged. I'm the proprietor of Earth's only interspecies bar.

Odd opportunities do come my way. "Vanayn said, 'Let's go for a ride.'"

"And you went?"

"Well, I didn't just—" Of course I'd been an idiot. "—didn't just jump up and run out to the ship. I asked, 'Can you bring me back here before the evening crowd?' And Vanayn said, 'Not a problem.'"

She looked behind her at Vanayn, a great gray-striped mass of muscle, big eyes and iron teeth under a bubble helmet. "Vanayn, now. He's a new species, isn't he?"

"Yeah. Predator, likes lots of room and not much company. Slow metabolism. Oxygen is a poison to him. He has his own ship. He came in behind the liner, *Quark Mapping*, following the neutrino trail.

"We were all at the big table, seven or eight species, when he came in. He steered a floating cargo bin around to the bar. I store foodstuffs for my alien customers, but the supplies have to get to me somehow. I stowed the tank and ran him up a drink. A bunch of the other aliens gathered around his table. I served them, and then we sat around talking for a while."

"About what?"

Familiar food was clearing my head. I still had to concentrate to remember. It was so long ago.

"Me," I said. "And the Tavern. My customers . . . the aliens, they're all temporary. Most of them are gone when the landers lift. A few stick around for a year or two. The humans who come in here, they're usually collecting data for a doctorate or a newsburst. So are my staff, all doctors and grad students, all here to learn something and then go write it up. The only permanent feature of the Draco Tavern is me."

She waited.

"Which makes sense," I said. "I'm at the heart of the

information flow. I was asked to go flying once before, and I turned that down." She started to interrupt, but I pushed on. "It was light-years away. Whatever they learn, it'll come back to the Draco Tavern. And I still couldn't make them see why I . . . don't . . . go anywhere."

"Drink," she said, and poured tea. "Shall I order something stronger?"

"Maybe an aquavit. Thank you."

"Does it satisfy you, this answer? The reason you don't travel?"

"Sure. Usually. I'd had a couple of Irish coffees, though. Then Vanayn said, 'Let me take you for a ride!' and I said, 'Can you get me back before the evening crowd?' And he said . . . damn."

"What?"

"He said, 'This is not a problem. I'll put us in a loop.' And all I had to do was ask him why."

"But you went."

"The way I saw it—well. Look around you."

We had tall and slender exoskeletal Chirpsithra. We had Gligstith(click)optok built like little gray tanks draped in green fur pelts. Bebebebeque arrayed around the rim of the table like big golden bugs. Finny entities drifted within a fishbowl on wheels. Funny featherless birds, Warblers, nested overhead.

Cheri Kaylor grinned. "I can identify most of these species."

I said, "Whatever they look like, whatever their shape, whatever they breath or drink or need for life support, I knew I was surrounded by folk who want me to continue in existence. If I was making a hideous mistake, one or another would point it out. If I had an accident, one or another would come rescue me."

"So you went."

"And they were all watching me. All these travelers who never turned down a dare. I took a moment to think it through, but how could I back down? Yeah, I went."

"Was it that same ship?" Kaylor asked. She was almost bouncing in her chair. "The one you landed in? It's not your standard lander."

"Looks something like a Taurus station wagon, doesn't it?"

"But big. How far can it go?"

"It's just a lander, Doctor. Lifeboat, Captain's gig, not the main ship."

"So it goes as far as the Moon?"

"At least. We were there in three hours. The gig kind of molded itself against the hull and Vanayn took me aboard."

Kaylor was starting to look puzzled.

"I watched him extrude a transparent bubble onto the hull," I said, "from the back of the control room. Now I was walled off, my life-support conditions and his, and a curved transparent wall between. He stripped out of his life-support gear. He's *odd* under that. And we took off," I said, "and everything turned weird."

"You didn't have much time for much weirdness," Kaylor said. "You were gone only seven hours."

"It was longer than that," I said. "Ship's time."

"You took off . . ."

"Earth and Moon shrank all in an instant, but so did the Sun. I don't know what kind of effect that was. 'What would you like to see?' Vanayn asked me.

" 'Saturn,' I said. I was remembering a starwatching party back in college, the first time I ever used a telescope. Mars was only a pink blotch, but Saturn never disappointed anyone. Vanayn didn't know the name, so I sketched the solar system to show him what I meant.

"Beyond the curved outer wall, the starscape turned to something stranger. 'Navigating through cf-furk-kup space isn't straightforward,' Vanayn said. My translator was having trouble with that word. 'The trick is to define the loop. Here, is that Saturn?'

" 'No,' I said.

Kaylor jumped. "Not Saturn?"

"No, it was a big, bloated gas giant planet. The ring was narrow, barely visible.

"Vanayn said, 'Okay, I can fix it.' His tentacles writhed, and the outside view changed. Graphs and letters in at least three dimensions. Probability curves, the infrared and X-ray universe, I had no idea what we were seeing. Later I learned to read some of those symbols—"

"Just a minute," Kaylor said. "Could this ship of yours have been traveling in time?"

"Oh, it was," I said. Aquavit had arrived, and I drank half of it and let it trickle down my throat. "Ah. Yeah, that's what Vanayn meant by 'put us in a loop.' The trick seems to be that you have to bring the ship back to the same point you left. Otherwise you've violated some important parity laws."

"You didn't learn that right away, though."

"Not for a couple of months. Mind, I didn't keep time very well. My watch racked up almost a year before the battery ran out."

"God, what an opportunity. But Saturn's rings aren't a permanent feature, Mr. Schumann. A moon bashes another moon or something, and for a few hundred thousand years we have big gaudy rings. Most of the time Saturn's rings must look a lot like Jupiter's or Neptune's."

I said, "Oh. But Vanayn thought he'd gotten lost."

"What happened then?"

"He started searching. He was trying to find the neutrino trail from *Quark Mapping*. First we went to a view of nothing but galaxies. Flat space, he said. That didn't do it. He took us to other domains, black holes, peculiar galaxies, always getting more and more lost.

"God, it was all wonderful! But it took weeks or months to

get anywhere. The displays didn't usually show normal space, normal suns and planets, or starscapes at all. Vanayn spent some time fiddling with my life support until I could get food—tee tee hatch nex ool means it won't kill me, whatever it tastes like, but I had to explain about vitamins and fiber. He showed me how to use his library. I did some research. Eventually I could read some of his displays.

"He was looking for the point in spacetime from which we'd left. It was the only way we could get back into the universe."

"Were you worried?"

"Scared out of my mind, at first. I was watching my life disappear. Vanayn never did consider himself lost. He was 'having an adventure.' I got on his nerves. Eventually Vanayn stopped talking to me.

"Then I kind of settled into the routine. I learned a lot from Vanayn's library. It was my only friend. It's sapient, near as I can tell. It taught me how to fiddle with the paste dispenser so I could get some variety into my diet. I made some changes in the medical system too. I invented two or three chemicals that would have a decent street value if I could manufacture them. After a while the library cut me off and made me sober up.

"I don't know how Vanayn worked out how to get us back. If that first planet really was Saturn a million years ago, or a million from now, or fifty, and if he figured that out . . . anyway, he still wasn't talking to me. He got us back to the Moon, and then he just pulled me into the gig and took us home."

"Wonderful," Cheri Kaylor said.

"Lettuce," I said. "David? When you get a minute, get me any kind of salad. I haven't eaten anything normal since . . . I still can't tell."

Magliocco hadn't said anything this whole time, but now he was looking at me like some sort of strange bug. He said, "It should have been me."

Cheri gave him a look: *Idiot!* He ignored her. "I've got credentials in cosmology and astronomy. He showed you sights the rest of the human race might never know. I might even have figured out what he was doing! Why a bartender?"

"I was the wrong man," I admitted. "You, Dr. Kaylor, any human being in here would have been a better choice. I just hate being lost."

I looked around at the evening crowd, a dozen assorted sizes and shapes, a whispering background of alien buzzes and clicks and screeching, seven or eight species from hundreds of light-years around. "I'm glad to be home."

Losing Mars

T he latest crop of visitors to Earth came rolling across the tundra: four shapeless bean bags glowing like psychedelic rainbows. They formed a queue and rolled through one of the low-and-wide airlocks, into the Draco Tavern. Two Chirpsithra turned from the bar and watched them approach.

It had been a quiet afternoon.

I spoke to the first bag to reach the bar. "Welcome to the Draco Tavern. What can I do for you?"

An insert on the bag spoke in the soft accents of a standard Chirpsithra translator system. "We seek to speak to any representative of the United Nations."

"There aren't any in tonight," I said. There rarely were, though it's not unheard of. "Is this urgent?"

"Of huge import, but our timeline is flexible," said another of the bags. "Rick Schumann the barkeep, can you contact the United Nations for us?"

"I can find somebody." I still had phone and e-mail codes for Cheri Kaylor and Carlos Magliocco.

"That is well. The Chirpsithra have demanded too high a fee

as mediators. Would you accept two-to-the-twentieth part of what we deal for?"

Less than a millionth? "I have no idea. What are we dealing for?"

"Mars."

I tapped out what Dr. Kaylor had scrawled on her card, and got her voice mail. "Cheri Kaylor. Leave your name, number, and vital statistics. An Arab slavemaster will contact you shortly."

That could hardly be her business office, I thought. "Rick Schumann, Draco Tavern. Some of my visitors have a strong interest in talking United Nations business—"

"Worth a trip to Siberia?" Dr. Kaylor had picked up.

"Worth more than that, I gather. I don't have the full details yet. Shall I call Mr. Magliocco too?"

"No, hold up, Rick. I'm actually *in* Siberia, in a bathtub at the Mount Forel Hotel. We can get Carlos involved if this looks interesting. Who's talking? What do they look like? Where are they from?" She sounded cheerful and intrigued.

"They haven't said. They're in full pressure gear. I think they're fish."

"Give me half an hour. I'll have an Irish coffee."

I hung up, wondering why she didn't want Magliocco. A bit of work-related rivalry?

Until the first alien lander came down thirty-six years ago, the United Nations had spent most of its time in internal bickering and grand theft. These days they presented more of a united front. Cheri Kaylor and Carlos Magliocco dealt with people like me, people who dealt directly with aliens.

The life-support bags were arrayed at a big table with two Chirpsithra and a bearlike creature who had walked down from the lander with not even an extra coat. Wen Goldsmith took their orders. The bags wanted water, any interesting flavor.

Okay, I'd guessed they were water dwellers. I poured them pitchers of tap water and glacier water to get them started, and I joined the circle. "Mars," I said.

"We are not involved," one of the Chirpsithra said. The other said, "We may be asked to judge."

One of the bags said, "We should wait for an official, should we not?"

"Dr. Kaylor will be here shortly," I said.

Another bag said, "We have no secrets. What would you have of us? We look like this." A picture formed on the bag's side: a deep sea eel with long, elaborated fins manipulating a keyboard, goggle eyes and prominent pink gills. "We dare not make this envelope transparent. There's too much light."

"You tell too much," the first bag said.

"They have not hidden themselves."

"I concede." The first bag showed a picture too, another deep sea eel, but with blue gills.

Dr. Kaylor came in. I'd never been sure of her rank, so I didn't give it. She sat at one of the floating chairs, flustered but not showing it much. "Welcome to the local neighborhood," she said.

"We are local indeed," Blue Gills said. "Neighbors. We are from Mars."

"Evolved on Europa," said Pink Gills.

"Colony established some thirty thousand years ago," said a third bag: Bronze Gills. The fourth still hadn't shown itself.

"Jupiter orbits, not Earth orbits."

"Are you aware of a near-frozen sea lying beneath the soil of Mars?"

"It covers near a hundred thousand square kilometers."

They waited. Dr. Kaylor said, "Yes, in Elysium, near the equa-tor. We think the dust keeps it from evaporating."

Blue Gills said, "Dust and rubble, then dust compressed to cement, then pack ice, then solid ice. The Elysium Sea is well pro-tected from loss of water vapor. Liquid water beneath. Conditions are very like those beneath the ice of Europa—"

"The increase in gravity is hard to notice." Pink Gills.

"Pressure increases faster with depth." Bronze Gills.

"But that's as well, as the Elysium Sea is more shallow."

Bronze Gills said, "Of course the taste of the water is quite dif-ferent. A bit of planet-shaping was needed, and still the taste—"

"We prefer it." Blue Gills.

"Barkeep, these are interesting flavors," Pink Gills said. "What else have you?"

"Want to try something carbonated? Cheri, I'll get your Irish coffee."

When I came back one of the bags was saying, "Years ago. Here a probe, there a probe, descended on Mars with no clear method or pattern. Some stayed in orbit, some landed, some struck hard. Half of them destroyed themselves or failed to send a signal. We saw a similarity in design and guessed that they were from the inner world."

"Yes, those were ours," Dr. Kaylor said.

"Then they stopped," said Blue Gills. "Nothing since three years ago. What happened?"

Cheri didn't speak, so I said, "The Chirpsithra ships started coming. We've learned more about the universe since then than throughout our whole history."

"But you ceased to explore Mars. Or did you cease entirely to explore?"

An uncomfortable silence. Cheri asked, "Did you come here in your own ship?"

Blue Gills said, "No! We feared you would take such as an invasion or violation of territory. When a Chirpsithra lander approached us, we concluded that we would be accepted as their guests. We come regarding a matter of territory, after all."

"Who owns Mars?" Pink Gills demanded.

"Well," said Cheri, "I don't speak for the United Nations. I can bring this to Hermes Padat, I think." The Secretary General.

Bronze Gills asked, "Can we settle this quickly? I myself dwell on Europa. Life support is a problem here. Too much gravity, too little pressure."

"Oh, no, a case like this could take years," Cheri said. "I should try to call the Secretary General."

In a stunned silence we watched Cheri dial.

One of the Chirpsithra said, "No. I think we can decide more quickly than that. We hold authority in this part of space. Dr. Kaylor, do you claim Mars?"

"Of course. It's our next-door neighbor, the nearest planet, much closer to us than Jupiter is."

"Do you currently build ships capable of reaching Mars?"

She swallowed. "Ah . . . no."

"Has any human being ever set foot on this neighbor planet?"

"No. We would have, but you came. You already own most of space, most of the galaxy. You've said so yourselves."

"Rick? Would you have gone to Mars if we had left you alone?"

When I was a boy, we had gone to the Moon, and come home, and stopped. Mars had changed whenever someone looked again, and always there was talk of putting a man there some day.

"I'm not sure."

"Fsst! I give Mars to the Europan colonists."

Cheri gulped. She said, "We will protest the decision."

"You have that right. Submit your protest to the ship, to *Safe*

Orbits, before our departure sixty-one days from today. Rick, bring us sparkers."

The rest stayed at the table, but Cheri Kaylor followed me to the bar. I asked, "Another drink?"

She spoke in a suppressed wail. "I've lost Mars!"

"Irish coffee?"

"What do I tell Hermes Padat? They'll never react in time. The UN can't decide to order dinner in sixty-one days! I've lost Mars! Yes, Irish coffee."

I talked while I worked. "Not by yourself. You didn't lose Mars without help. Mars has been there all along. For hundreds of years we've known we could get there. For fifty years we've even known how. It just wasn't important enough to enough people. We never had Mars in the first place."

"They aren't even Martians. I wouldn't mind being kicked off by Martians."

"They didn't seem to mind the probes. Maybe they'll *want* visitors."

"And if they don't?"

"Cheri, how much territory is a millionth of Mars?"

"Why?"

"It's my commission. It might be enough for an embassy."

It turns out to be around a hundred and forty square kilometers.

PLAYGROUND EARTH

It was wonderfully peaceful in the dark beneath Europa's ice. The VR setup saw in infrared. The little scooter tootled among schools of alien swimmers lit by their own heat. Most of them looked like translucent squid or ambulatory jet engines. One variety had carved the underside of the ice into channels and buildings, a whole inverted city.

I had put my life on hold while recovering from a chain of misfortunes.

A Chirpsithra, Diplomat-by-Choice Ktashisnif, had died of allergies while in custody of human kidnappers. The perps had been turned over to the crew of *Transstar Code,* and the Chirps had executed them in the same way Ktashisnif had died, by slow suffocation. In a flurry of bad publicity, *Transstar Code* had departed Earth and Sol system and left me holding the bag.

I'd closed the Draco Tavern. I had little choice.

Wandering Signal took up orbit around the Moon a month later. Various diplomats inside and outside the UN attempted to stop the ship from sending landers. They may have been too subtle, and nobody fired any weapons at visiting aliens, though we'd worried about that.

The landers the Chirpsithra use are nowhere near the size of their interstellar liners, but they're big and conspicuous. It may be a good thing that Mount Forel is so inaccessible; the ship got its share of news cameras anyway. And someone mailed a package to the Draco Tavern that turned out to be a bomb.

Some of us were inside doing maintenance. The bomb killed another Chirpsithra, Engineer Hrashantree, and left me with internal injuries. It would have hurt a lot more of us if the Tavern hadn't been closed.

In the weeks that followed I sat or lay around being entertained by little sensor packages that various aliens have been sending out among the planets. The proxies crawl or swim across most of the interesting places in the solar system. Departing Chirpsithra liners don't bother to collect them; the next starship just links up, and Earth's satellite network have access too.

Mars was fun for a while, but there weren't any life-forms to make the place interesting. Pluto and Charon hosted actual tourists wearing video cameras and other sensors, entities who could never visit Earth. Jupiter was just confusing. Europa—

My virtuals went black and jerked me from under the Europan ice, back into my bedroom. I blinked and tried to sit up. "Beth?"

"You have friends," Beth Marble said.

"I've got lots of friends." I sat up, lifting mostly with my arms; but my belly muscles were growing back together. Soon, leg lifts.

Beth said, "Your friends in lobster shells that are too tall for the ceilings. Can they come in?"

"Chirpsithra. Sure, bring 'em in."

Beth Marble had gotten a raw deal. She'd been a psychiatric

technician taking care of developmentally disabled patients until, in her mid-thirties, she'd opted to work with minds more alien than that. She'd put in for work at the Draco Tavern. She was lucky the bomb hadn't caught her. Now she was taking care of me until we could get the Tavern rolling again.

She came back with a pair of Chirpsithra. At eleven feet tall they entered crouched over, and immediately sat on the floor. Beth took the reading chair.

"I wish I had better hospitality to offer," I said. "I don't even have sparkers for you."

"Travel involves occasional discomfort. If need sparkers or to straighten up, we return to the lander," one said in Lottl. "I am Shastrastinth, this is Stachun. How is your health?"

"Much improved. I would have been crippled without Gligstith(click)optok medical assistance." I wondered how much the Glig had learned of human physiology that way, then dismissed the thought. They'd studied human tourists on their own world; they had our DNA.

I asked, "How are your passengers?"

"Restless. Some have decided to travel." She was still speaking Lottl. Beth's translator was on. I reached for mine.

"I saw some of that on the news," Beth said. "Gligstith . . . the gray ones built like little walking tanks. They wear green furs? They've been visiting hospitals. And the wolflike things—"

Unease crawled up my rebuilt spine. "Tell me more."

Following the explosion there had been a period of dithering on the part of *Wandering Signal*'s crew and passengers, matched by dithering from the United Nations. Various diplomats were trying not to admit that they didn't want aliens running loose across the Earth. Others, isolationists and Muslim and Christian fundamentalists, were screaming their heads off, but they've been doing that since the first ship was sighted.

Chirpsithra crew and their varied passengers had done some touring even when the Draco Tavern was available to keep them occupied. Funds that would have repaired the Tavern after the bomb had dried up. Meanwhile sixty or seventy aliens of a dozen species—I was guessing a little here—had been sitting in *Wandering Signal*'s lander, possibly waiting for an engraved invitation that wasn't going to come.

Then I'd stopped watching the news.

Shastrastinth said, "The Mnemoposh have caused disturbances. They never come out of the lander, but they explore virtually. Their probes look like miniature selves, and they are large enough to be noticed. Some of your kind fear large insects."

"I do." Beth hadn't told me that when she signed up for the Tavern. "Most of the probes are this size," the size of her thumb. "Tens of thousands of them, wandering all over the Earth."

"Not conspicuous," Shastrastinth said.

"CNN has videotapes."

"These are complex machines, for all of their size," said Shastrastinth. "Many include projectors and translator-speakers."

Beth said, "A lot of people have seen big metal-and-plastic bugs. In Africa and the Mideast they think the Americans make them. Now the Gligstith," she clicked her tongue, "*them*, they've started visiting hospitals."

Shastrastinth said, "We have no good sense how your folk will react to our renewed presence. They rioted when we executed Ktashisnif's killers. That surprised us. We hoped you might help us understand."

I said, "Seven billion people go in seven billion directions. I don't predict human behavior any better than I do yours. Do you think you can persuade the Mnemoposh to give interviews? I don't mind what they look like as long as they're willing to talk about what they've seen on Earth. Get them to act like tourists until they aren't news anymore."

"We may ask," the alien said.

"What about the Glig? Visiting hospitals doesn't sound bad."

Beth said, "Most hospitals won't let them in, most countries. They took a tour through St. John's in Santa Monica. NBC followed them around with cameras. They scare some of the patients. They dropped a lot of hints. Some doctors on TV are talking about big changes in medical practice. Others don't like it."

Some doctors would have trouble keeping up, and they wouldn't like changes. I said, "That sounds generally good. What about the Folk?"

"The ones like wolves with their heads on upside down?"

"That's them."

Beth was repressing a shudder. I was starting to wonder if the Draco Tavern was really her thing. She said, "They're annoying the hell out of police departments in various countries."

"Sure, they're hunters. They're trying to hunt down the bomber."

"Well, they've been collecting people. Arresting them. I'm sorry you got hurt, Rick, but how many bombers can they get for one bomb?"

"How many have they got?"

"I think . . . eleven. Some of them are on the FBI and CIA terror lists. And the Folk won't talk to anyone about it."

"Yet again, that sounds like the problem," I said. "Talk them into giving interviews, Shastrastinth."

"Folk don't talk well. We thought an intermediary would be best. You, Rick Schumann."

"I'm not up to it." It may be I'd needed a vacation, or even a few weeks in a rest home, even before the bomb went off. I'd grown tired of my role as bartender to aliens. Strange shapes and sizes and odors and diets don't bother me after all these years, but for the moment I just couldn't face being tossed back into that storm of controversy and misunderstandings, alien viewpoints and mind-bending surprises.

I asked, "What are your other passengers doing? Anything that hasn't been noticed?"

"No," said Shastrastinth.

Stachun spoke for the first time. "Wastlubl is loose."

"Wastlubl is inconspicuous," Shastrastinth said.

Suddenly I was feeling wiped out. I said, "Tell you what, I'll start watching news again. My translator can reach you, right? I'll call you if anything occurs to me."

So I immersed myself in the news. I ran the TV while Beth had me on physical therapy, and while I ate, and while I slept. My mind was still a little mushy. It took me a couple of days to catch up.

The Folk had arrested twelve people. Two of those were French, six were Saudi, the rest were random and hard to place. The Folk made no secret of their activities, but they didn't talk either; they just swooped, swept the locality with some kind of stun beam, and grabbed.

Aliens toured the Louvre: a smooth-skinned flightless bird guiding a floating table that carried ten golden bugs ten inches tall. I recognized the Bebebebeque, but not the bird. Cameras followed them as they explored, the bird croaking questions at a bewildered French escort.

An oversized entity was visiting landmarks: the pyramids of Egypt and Mexico, Mount Rushmore, Rome and Tokyo. I watched her looming over a camera crew at the St. Louis Arch.

I called the lander.

"Shastrastinth, I don't know what you call conspicuous," I said. "There's an alien your height, built like a big-headed mantis, three jaws for a mouth, talks to anyone at all—"

"Tenjer is child of a species whose adults cannot travel," she said. "She's seeking Wastlubl, her . . . pet, instructor, playmate, toy. They're playing hide-and-seek. Wastlubl will set ever more difficult puzzles while Tenjer tries to find it."

"Child. Okay. Tenjer seems bright enough—"

"The child is intelligent. Adults are even more so. Is Tenjer giving enough interviews to satisfy you?"

"Sure, the kid just doesn't make much sense. Now, was it you who got the Folk talking?"

"I asked them to be more interactive."

If that was a mistake, it was mine. I said, "One of their . . . prey has confessed to blowing up the Tavern. Amory Saloman, American, wants to sell the story to NBC. The Folk don't want to let him go."

"Problem will solve itself if we wait. Can he talk from his confinement?"

"I'm not his agent. Let them thrash it out on their own. Now, what's going on in the ocean around Hawaii?"

"I did expect those to be inconspicuous. The Sea People hail from a world much like your own, but lack exposed continents. Would you wish to swim with them? Some adults wear sensor gear; you can use a virtual link."

". . . Maybe later. Adults? Are they breeding?" Complaints had been reported from fishermen: their catch was being depleted.

"Their progeny will be unsapient and sterile. One generation only."

"What do they eat?"

"They eat what they find in the sea."

"It would help if you could get the Sea People to keep their numbers down."

"We will ask."

"Next. Do you know anything about a Dianna Gustal? She's claiming contact with an alien."

"One of our passengers?"

Who else? There *weren't* any other aliens. Then again, the woman sounded crazy. "Her alien seems to be the fount of all wisdom. It's been everywhere, done everything, seen every interesting moment in human history. Trouble is, I've heard Chirpsithra talk like that. Is there one of your people who just can't stand not talking to the natives?"

"Shrug. Rick, our concern is to keep the peace. What threatens the peace here?"

"Don't know. I'm glad the Folk are doing their job. They'll find the worst threats." I wasn't sure of what I was saying. Watching the Folk in action could scare a lot of people over the edge.

They put me on physical therapy. It would have been hellish, but I remembered worse. I remembered being unable to move at all, back a few weeks ago.

The Sea People took action to improve their image. With the help of a Venezuelan company, they did underwater work to set up an OTEC power plant. It would use the temperature difference between surface water and bottom water in the ocean to make electric power. The side effect: currents would stir up sea bottom soil. More trace elements in the water. More fish.

I hoped some of Earth's six billion would understand its purpose and take it as a kindness. Still, the Sea People, when they finally appeared on television, were shocking. They were eels, their streamlining ruined by a collar of limbs and a tremendous toothy head. Beth didn't like them at all. Earth's fish and crustaceans can be surpassingly ugly, but they couldn't match the Sea People.

Yet the virtual link to the Sea People became hugely popular, especially in hospitals and rest homes. I tried it myself. I loved the dreamy feel of effortless swimming.

Dianna Gustal announced that her alien contact was—or had once been—Elvis Presley.

People around the world started seeing bugs the size of a ten-year-old child. I called the lander. Yes, they were hologram projections of the Mnemoposh.

Shastrastinth had a word with them. Now witnesses began seeing transparent people who talked like stand-up comics. That didn't go over well either. *The Tonight Show* host, Jay Leno's successor, started talking about Biblical plagues.

I was yanked away from the dark blue deeps off Maui. "What?" I demanded.

"Human on the phone," Beth said, with composure. "From Washington, D.C. Says he's with the Secretary General's office."

One Harold Macy wanted me to meet him at the Draco Tavern. He couldn't say exactly what for. I agreed because I was becoming a little stir-crazy.

We put my motor chair in the SUV, and Beth drove us over the tundra.

Macy looked like an actor, tall, square jaw, intense green eyes, wonderful blond-going-gray hair. He looked around at the row of airlocks in front of the Tavern. Damage wasn't visible from here. "That doesn't look bad," he said.

"Sonic shields took some of the force. Most of the damage is inside," I said, "toward the back."

So I took the chair through the big airlock and we toured the inside. Macy's nose wrinkled at the interesting chemicals released first by the explosion, then by what was happening to the various foodstuffs stored here. We should have moved those outside.

I hadn't wanted to see what the bomb had done. It was bad: not just the shattered booths, but darkness and mildew, the magic lost because of lost power, the dead feel to the place. Yet

I felt a fierce pride. I'd built this over half my life span. This was mine.

The spa took Macy's attention. "Do you need this?"

I'd put it in when I had some spare money. I said, "Sometimes a customer uses it. The Zash held a mating ceremony in there." They'd invited me and Corinne to join them. "It needs a lot of cleaning. We can't use chlorinated anything."

"What would it cost to—"

"Nothing. It didn't get damaged."

He nodded. "How much to repair *all* the damage?"

"We're guessing thirty billion dollars."

"That sounds like a lot."

"Could be more. Let's go around back," I said.

I tried my motor chair on the icy paths, and found it good. The back of the Draco Tavern was a row of plug-in toilets.

"Here." I opened one that the Qarashteel used. It looked like a miniature chemical factory and smelled like one too. Macy shied back. I asked, "Can you see any damage?"

"No."

"I can't either. They say it's a total loss. I understand some of what makes the Tavern work, at least well enough that I don't poison anyone, but these toilets are a mystery. Doesn't matter, they're all plug-ins. The users bring their own. But the interfaces are all up against the back wall, so the explosion ruined a lot of them. I lost half my booths too, sonic dampers, translators—the news anchors talk about Hrashantree's death and my injuries, but a translator network died too. That's an intelligent being. We'd need a volunteer to replace it. Thirty billion is just a guess."

"Okay."

"What?"

Macy opened his briefcase. "I brought a contract."

"Who's supposed to pay for this?"

"Officially, it's the Emergency Funds Office branch of the United Nations. There were assessments and contributions. Your aliens can be really annoying, you know? It's not that we want to live without them. They've been changing civilization, the knowledge they bring in, and it's usually for the better. But we'd rather they stay here, most of the time, anyway. The, uh, fish? You could feed them here, can't you?"

"That bomb blew up my aquarium. Otherwise, sure, except that they've been breeding. They don't do that when they don't have room."

"And that Godzilla-sized kid and his toy. It'd be easier to catch if it didn't have the run of the whole planet."

The Tavern was too small for that kind of chasing around. "How about confining them to just the Mount Forel environment?"

"Whatever. What are you doing?"

I was crossing out clauses in his contract. "I don't want to give away the Tavern!"

"They won't go for it."

"I'll keep my autonomy, thank you very much. Why in Hell would I submit to inspection by—" By people just out of the Stone Age, if that clause were strictly enforced. Always look a gift horse in the mouth. "I'm still healing, Mr. Macy. I don't really want to go back to work yet. Give the Emergency Funds Office some time to talk it over."

"Mmm."

"Want to try something? Chignthil Interstellar sells a liqueur called Opal Fire."

During the next two weeks ahi, mahi, and swordfish went off the menus in most restaurants.

Elvis Presley revealed a list of commandments—and Shastrastinth caught the pair who had been manipulating that poor woman. Dianna Gustal had been communicating with a Mnemo-posh hologram, and that worthy had been getting its cues from a Vollek merchant ready to sell a new religion.

A big-headed mantis eleven feet tall, with a three-jawed mouth armed with dagger teeth, chased its giggling prey through the Northridge Mall in California. The damage was more spec-tacular than expensive. Chirpsithra negotiators offered to pay for repairs.

The Mnemoposh opened access to their bug-sized cameras to the Fox network for an undisclosed sum. Other networks merged forces and sued.

The Folk held their hunt. By Chirpsithra law it had to be tele-vised. Their prisoners—minus two, released as innocent—were set loose all at once, and that allowed them to form bands, set traps, and swarm the occasional Folk. They'd have held out longer if they hadn't needed water. The Folk lost two, the prisoners lost all. There was a storm of protest—

And my funding came through.

I've been able to open up part of the Tavern while repairs go on. We beefed up our security: it's harder to get in than it used to be. Beth Marble surprised me: she gets along best with the weirdest of my customers. Shapes don't bother her unless they resemble Earth's more noxious life-forms, and the oddest of alien minds are still saner than what she was used to at the hospital.

Beyond that it's been business as usual at the Draco Tavern.